"Cian MacFarlane is one of the most complex and fascinating characters I've ever read in a book. This book has it all—turn the page suspense, a story of the bond between brothers, betrayals, secrets, and romance. BREATH of DECEIT is Selena Laurence at her finest." - *Sandra Owens, author of the best-selling K2 Team and Aces & Eights series.*

"Laurence's tightly woven story is a superb mix of sexual and political tension that's certain to please fans of both." — *Publisher's Weekly review of The Kingmaker*

"Selena Laurence has the ability to bring to life complex characters you instantly start rooting for from page one." — *Ilsa Madden-Mills, Wall Street Journal Bestselling Author on Buried*

Also by Selena Laurence

The Powerplay Series
Prince of the Press
The Kingmaker
POTUS
SCOTUS
The Darkhorse

BRUSH OF DESPAIR

Dublin Devils 2

SELENA LAURENCE

everafter ROMANCE

Prologue

"Hey," Cian murmured into the phone as he stood in the dark. "Give me just a sec." He looked at the brunette still sleeping in the bed and couldn't help but smile softly to himself. After making his way out of the bedroom, down the hall, and into the living room, he opened a set of sliding glass doors and stepped out onto a large balcony. Years ago, when his father and brother had been arrested, the *Chicago Tribune* had done an exposé on the MacFarlanes. The reporter had dubbed him the *Irish Prince of the Windy City*. It was one of the few good laughs Cian's inner circle had gotten during those trying times. His brothers Finn and Connor had called him *Your Highness* for weeks afterward.

But standing here now, Connor on the phone and safe thousands of miles away, Lila Rodriguez sleeping in his bed, and the lights of Chicago laid out below him, he did feel like a prince, albeit a dark and damned one.

"Tell me your new life is everything you dreamed," Cian said.

"It is, and a lot more," Connor answered. "We're doing great, the place I'm managing is great, and my *roommate* gets a new assignment every couple of weeks, but she seems to love that."

"And you're meeting people? Making friends or whatever?" Cian chuckled.

He could hear the smile in Connor's voice when he answered. "Yes, Mom, we're making friends with the other kids."

There was a pause as Cian held a deep breath and let it go. He closed his eyes and pictured Connor in the sunshine, and his heart expanded.

"But how are things there?" Connor asked.

"Nothing you need to worry about. Just more of the same."

"And is he looking for us?" Connor asked softly.

They both knew *he* almost certainly was. Robbie MacFarlane was never going to let one of his sons go without a fight, but Cian gave the answer Connor needed to hear for now. "Haven't heard a word about it," Cian assured his brother. "Ma is keeping him busy with projects around the house. I've never seen the old man so hog-tied."

"I miss you guys," Connor said plainly.

Cian watched the lights of a plane blink rapidly as it flew far overhead. It too was on its way to freedom, the freedom Connor had, the freedom Cian would purchase for Liam and Finn, the freedom he so very much wanted to give to Lila. "We miss you too. More than words can say. But this is right. This is what I've always wanted for you, and I couldn't be more proud."

"I don't think I can ever…" Connor began.

"Don't. You don't have to, I don't need you to. Just live and be happy."

There was another pause, and Cian knew his brother's heart was full and there was so much more both of them wanted to say. But as with everything in his life, he felt the grinding pressure of a timer counting down.

"It's time," he told Connor. "You get Finn next. Look for the number tomorrow."

"Okay. *Slán abhaile.*"

"*Slán abhaile*," Cian replied.

After disconnecting, he dismantled the phone, crushed the SIM card beneath the edge of a heavy potted plant, and threw it over the side of the balcony. He leaned stiff armed on the railing, the air cold against his bare chest. A wry smile spread across his lips as he thought again of the nickname. He might be the Irish Prince, but the city was very windy, and it was blowing straight for him.

Chapter One

Six Weeks Later

"You'll do it because I told you to," Lila snapped into the mic on her laptop.

"And if I want to hear it straight from Xavier himself?" the man on the other end of the line asked.

"Then I'll tell you you're done at Rogue," she said, her tone switching from irritated to bored. "It doesn't make much difference to me. I can hire another dozen as good or better than you in about fifteen minutes. Just make up your mind, because I'm too busy to keep playing this game with you."

The man said some choice words, mostly aimed at her gender, then disconnected the communication. Lila sighed, her brow furrowed in concentration as she punched keys on her computer, signing into a highly encrypted account before typing a series of numbers that eliminated the man's access to the dark website Rogue, where he'd worked until sixty seconds earlier. Then, for good measure, with a few more keystrokes, she pulled up his personal bank account and removed half the balance, transferring it to the local domestic violence shelter.

"Now who's the cunt?" she muttered to herself.

If someone had told her a few weeks ago that she'd be running Rogue and dealing with issues like hiring and firing in addition to the technical aspects, she'd never have believed them.

But here she was, and she had to admit, she was getting the hang of it.

The internal Rogue chat box popped up, and she read the message:

Client in Argentina is asking if we'd consider listing some items for them like we are for our Irish friends.

Lila looked at the screen, her mind flipping through the background and options. The Irish friends referred to the Dublin Devils, Chicago mobsters who were run by Lila's sometime lover, Cian MacFarlane. Rogue sold drugs on the dark web for Cian and his brothers, and while the process had run smoothly so far, Lila had to admit the world in general had gotten a lot more complicated since they'd gone into business with the Devils.

Lila knew firsthand what getting into bed with drug dealers meant, and Rogue's Argentinean client wasn't known for his stability in business or anywhere else. Just the previous year, he'd started augmenting his black market cryptocurrency business with arms dealing and attracted the ire of the 'Ndrangheta, the Argentine mafia. Lila had worked hard to keep the client's accounts safe when the 'Ndrangheta had launched their best cyberterrorists at Rogue. At the time, Lila had been Rogue's top hacker and security specialist, not the boss, so she hadn't thought much about other possible repercussions to the event.

And now he was asking her to enable him to compete directly with her main client, Cian.

She looked at the clock on her living room wall. There were clocks and timers on her devices; she wasn't sure why she'd always kept the strange old manual-wind clock on the wall. She had to take it down every twenty-four hours and wind it; it was ugly and lost three seconds every hour, making it perpetually slow. Yet, she rewound and reset it once a day and kept it hanging there right above her desk.

Lila hadn't been running Rogue long, and she had always thought of herself as a cautious person, yet in the last year, she'd begun to realize her view of herself wasn't very honest. Because Lila had spent most of her life taking risks, if she were being honest. And while she kept certain aspects of her life as safe as possible, to the point of being dull—her social life, for instance—in a lot of other things, she took risks every day.

Since she'd been barely out of high school, Lila had been earning her way in the world as a hacker. She helped criminals commit crimes, and in the process of doing that, she'd committed a whole bunch of crimes herself. And until a few months ago, she'd somehow thought that was safe because the crimes were virtual, the work associates were as well, and, after all, she lived in a boring row house in a dully gentrified neighborhood a short distance from Chicago's downtown.

Then she'd been assigned to help the Dublin Devils sell opiates on the web, and her carefully constructed image of herself had been crumbling ever since. She'd managed to get crossways in her boss Xavier's business with the Russian Bratva, then she'd gone and slept with Cian MacFarlane, helped hide Cian's brother Connor from their father, and agreed to take over the management of Rogue after she'd accidently killed Xavier.

Yeah, it was safe to say Lila wasn't actually a cautious woman at all.

But really, Lila thought as she toggled her screen back to what she'd been working on—a list of Robbie MacFarlane's hidden assets—it shouldn't be such a surprise to her, this newfound risky streak. She'd been raised at the knee of a compulsive gambler and had spent most of her adolescence helping good old Dad cheat his way to whatever profits he could.

No, Lila had begun to realize that the choices she'd been making most of her adult life were based in a lot of risk-taking behavior, and, in fact, she'd begun to wonder if she'd inherited the gambling gene and hacking was merely her personal manifestation of it.

She switched the screen again, reading the message one more time. It was definitely a gamble if she agreed to the Argentine client's newest request. And Lila had no interest in gaining either Cian's ire or the 'Ndrangheta's notice. Yet, she had to admit she was intrigued. Could she find a way to filter the retail pages so they'd be seen by a different audience than for the products she sold for Cian and the Devils? Could she manipulate by geography and browsers in such a way that clients never saw more than one seller's product? There were plenty of drug users to go around, she reasoned with herself. Maybe she'd just run a few tests, try a few things out in private.

Once she'd found a way to make it work, she could run it by Cian. Yes, maybe Lila was a gambler after all. And now she was gambling with more than simply a livelihood. Lila was gambling with lives.

**

Cian's footsteps were nearly silent on the worn wood floors of the darkened hallway. A soft popping sound next to him had his heart racing before he realized it was one of the refrigeration units in the commercial kitchen behind the nearest door.

"Fuck," he muttered under his breath.

He made his way down the hallway until he reached the metal back door that led onto the alley behind his club, Banshee. It was four a.m., and his guard detail were entertaining themselves with a game of poker at the bar up front, the place having closed two hours ago.

He pressed the handle on the door and quietly slid outside, pushing a chunk of brick with his foot so it blocked the door from closing and locking him out. Then he made his way down the alley, staying close to the building where the shadows kept him somewhat camouflaged.

"You alone?" he asked when he saw the outline of the man leaning against the back wall of the office building that shared the alley with Banshee.

"Yep. Just me tonight," the figure answered, stepping away from the wall and into the overhead light, revealing him to be Don Wagner, FBI agent.

Cian gave his shoulders a quick roll, squaring his stance as he stopped in front of Don. He reached into the pocket of his leather jacket and extracted a USB drive.

"Why'd you want it this way?" he asked Don, watching the other man's expression carefully.

Don was the smarter of the two agents Cian had been informing to for the last three plus years. A mid-sized man with thinning dark hair, cheap suits, and an utterly forgettable face, Don was cautious where his partner tended towards reckless, but Don was also ambitious where Bruce was lazy. Cian's informing had started as a way to keep his brother Liam out of prison, and now the feds had him by the balls, and Cian spent much of his time trying to outlast the bastards. He had three younger brothers, and that meant three men he needed to get out of the mob. So far, he'd managed one. He'd play with the feds for another decade if it meant he saved the other two.

"Our security guys say there've been some breaches of our systems. We have to be extra cautious for a while until they figure it out."

Cian rolled his lips together to keep from smirking. At least one of those breaches had been the handiwork of Lila Rodriguez, his favorite genius. At the thought of Lila, Cian's chest tightened. Then he pushed the thoughts aside. Lila was another problem for another day.

He handed the USB drive to Don. "This has photos of Consuelos and his guys taking a shipment from the Martinez cartel last week. It also has a list of locations where they keep their product. It's current as of thirty-six hours ago. If you raid ASAP, it'll probably still be there. If you wait a week for some damn piece of paperwork to get filed, the stuff will be long gone."

Don's eyes narrowed as he dropped the drive

into the breast pocket of his cheap suit jacket.

"Where's the info on the Devils, Cian? I've been waiting for weeks now. Connor's *vacation* was arranged by me," Don said. "You owe me."

Cian debated whether to play it tough or sympathetic. He usually went with tough when dealing with the feds, but decided to change it up this time.

"Look," he said, dipping his head as he ran a hand over the back of his neck. "Connor running set the old man off with a vengeance."

Don snorted. "As if you couldn't have seen that coming."

"Yeah, but he has everything battened down so tight right now I'm lucky if I can log into a computer to send an email without a guard looking over my shoulder. Robbie blames me for Connor taking off and he's not giving me an inch."

"And why should I give a damn?" Don retorted.

"Because my old man has a short attention span," Cian lied through his teeth. Robbie was like a bulldog and never forgot a single slight. He also had a head that remembered business details almost as well as Cian's did. "As soon as some crisis or battle crops up, he'll be off after that shiny. Give it a few weeks, and I'll be free to get you whatever you want. I just need to lay low right now."

Don watched him closely and Cian held the other man's gaze, his expression as bland as he could make it.

"Don't fuck this up for me, Cian," Don warned. "This is my ticket up the ladder, and if you ruin it, I'll make it my life's work to ruin you."

"Have a nice night, Don," Cian drawled before

he turned on his heel and walked away. As he slipped back in the door to Banshee, he finally took the deep breath he'd been craving, the one that meant he was still alive, heart still pumping, muscles still moving. Body and brain still functioning, still working to save his brothers.

Then he did what he did at the end of every day—he closed his eyes and asked God to give him just one more.

**

"Tell them I'm going to be at O'Neil's alone," Cian instructed Lila as she sat watching him over a table at Starbucks in Wicker Park.

The place was crammed with its usual assortment of millennial entrepreneurs— actors working on their portfolios, commodities brokers researching their next trade, college students pretending to study.

And one mobster meeting with one world-class hacker to discuss the Russian Bratva.

"And will you?" she asked, looking skeptical.

Cian chuckled. "What do you think?"

"I think you shouldn't be baiting them and you shouldn't be in the same place they are if you can avoid it." Her lips tightened, and he noted that today, she wore raspberry lipstick. Shiny, as always. Tempting, also per the norm. It had been weeks since she'd slept in his bed, and honestly, by now he'd expected her to be long gone, but her mother had been diagnosed with cancer before he could get Lila out of the country, and now she refused to budge while her mom was undergoing treatment.

Her delicate features creased as she leaned

forward and whisper-shouted at him. "They're dangerous, and they have no sense of humor. Why would you voluntarily let them get near you?"

He smiled benignly at her. It warmed his heart to know she cared about what happened to him. Generally, his brothers were the only people who gave a damn. To everyone else, he was a means to an end—an ATM to his employees, a weapon to be wielded against others by his father, a tool for prying open Chicagoland crime to the FBI.

"I appreciate the concern," he told her genuinely. "But my men are the best. They won't let anything happen. We'll have home field advantage on our side as well as the element of surprise."

"Why do you want to go face-to-face with them?" she asked, leaning back in her chair, slightly stiff, her cheeks pinking up in anger.

He lowered his voice as he reached out to run a finger along her exposed wrist. He saw her eyes flare with surprise, but she didn't pull away. Yes, they'd slept together—more than once—no, it didn't mean they *were* together.

"I need to get a feel for who I'm dealing with. All the research and dirt in the world can't compare to what I'll learn looking one of their men in the eyes. I need to know what they're doing here, what they're after, and how they plan to get it. But more than that, I need to know where the chinks are in their armor and how they deal with other people. That will tell me how to proceed."

She scowled at him. "Fine. When should I tell them you'll be there?"

"This afternoon, two p.m. Tell them you've been tapping in to my texts. Don't give them an exact address for O'Neil's. You don't want to seem too up in my business."

Lila nodded. "Is that everything?"

He watched her, the tense set of her shoulders, the way she wouldn't look him in the eye. He didn't like it, but for now, he couldn't change it.

"Yes. Is everything else going okay?"

"It's fine. Sales are solid. We seem to have settled into some patterns. Certain days and products are doing better." She paused. "And I have something related to ask you about, something another client is wanting, but I'll wait until I see if it's even possible."

"Okay, whenever you're ready, ask away." He smiled some more, hoping to thaw her out. But it was met with silence and a dead gaze. "So should we phase out the losers?" he finally asked, mentally giving up—for now.

"Yes, the more we can prune, the less chance of problems arising. Streamline everything to the top earners, then if something new comes along that we think might work, we can always do some pilot projects."

You'd think she was discussing the sale of magazines or jewelry rather than drugs. Lila was not only a genius with a computer, she was a damn good businesswoman.

"Sounds fine to me. You want to give Finn a list of what to cut? So we can alter our purchasing." He raised an eyebrow at her, and she looked away from him again.

Then she did that thing she'd always done, stood abruptly, obviously out of whatever patience or forbearance she needed to deal with him. It was puzzling, but he'd begun to accept it.

"Maybe next week. I'll go send the message right away."

"Thank you," he told her, rising from his own seat in a more relaxed fashion. "Does your mother have another doctor's appointment today?"

She nodded, swinging her messenger bag onto one shoulder.

"You'll tell me if either of you needs anything?"

"Yes. Thank you."

She turned to leave, and he couldn't stop himself from reaching out and grabbing her elbow. She looked at him over her shoulder, and her eyes nearly undid him. "I care, Lila from Rogue," he murmured, his gaze burning into hers, holding her trapped as her lips parted and he saw her breath quicken. "I'm not able to give you what you deserve, but I care, and I'll always be here."

She blinked at him, then gently pulled her arm from his grasp before turning her back and walking away from him.

He thought he might never get used to watching people he cared for walk away.

Chapter Two

Katerina Zima Volkova opened her eyes to darkness. An oppressive and overwhelming darkness. It was only because she could hear breathing that she knew she wasn't alone. Even though they were all jammed into the small space, there was no light anywhere, and she couldn't see the body closest to hers no matter how much she strained her eyes.

"Nadja," she whispered, digging her elbow into soft flesh. "Nadja." She elbowed her neighbor again.

"*Ukhodi!*" Nadja mumbled, slapping at Katerina's elbow. *Go away.*

"*Nyet. Vstavay,*" Katerina replied. *Wake up.*

Nadja cursed and moved. Katerina could feel her friend sitting up next to her.

"What do you want?" Nadja snapped as someone across the room shushed them both.

"We need to try to get out of here," Katerina whispered. "There are only two men in the hall, and they're asleep. This may be our chance."

Nadja sighed, and the resignation in that one small sound sent Katerina's anger spinning to the surface.

"We're not giving up," she gritted out beneath her breath.

"Katya," Nadja said softly as she placed a hand on Katerina's arm. "They are too powerful, too strong. They will find us, and it will be so much worse."

"Worse than being forced to service filthy men in an even filthier brothel?" Katerina snapped. "Worse than being told when we can and can't eat, bathe, use the bathroom? Worse than never seeing friends or family again?"

Nadja snorted softly in the pitch black. "It's already too late for that."

Katerina tried not to think about the moment earlier in the day when the men had chosen Nadja to take away. Every day they chose a handful of women in the room and took them away, bringing them back several hours later. Sometimes the women were beaten, sometimes they were crying. Some hadn't spoken since they'd returned. And Nadja had come back with glassy eyes and slurred words. She'd mumbled something at Katya, then fallen asleep on the bare, dirty mattress they shared. When she'd woken a few hours later, she'd pasted on a big smile and said to Katya, "Now get the cards back out, because I was winning."

Katerina tentatively put her hand out, meeting up with Nadja's knee. She gave it a quick squeeze, then whispered, "If we get away it doesn't have to happen again."

"Katya." Nadja cupped the back of Katerina's

head and drew their foreheads together. "I've seen these men. There is no getting away."

Then she lay back down, murmuring for Katerina to get some sleep, because they never knew when the men would come again.

Katerina stared into the darkness, hearing the women around her as they slept, dreamed, cried. Some prayed quietly to themselves; others whispered to one another like she and Nadja. She breathed deeply of the odor of sweat and fear. How long would they be kept here like this, she wondered. And how many more opportunities would they have to escape before they were taken someplace even worse?

Something in Katerina's gut told her a window of opportunity was closing, but she wouldn't leave Nadja, no matter what. They'd planned to move to America together, filling out the applications that their friend Jakob had given them for jobs as hostesses. They didn't know what hostesses were, but Jakob said it was working in restaurants, making the diners feel comfortable. "It's easy work," he'd said. "They like pretty girls who can smile."

Katerina and Nadja had been thrilled. They were young, they were pretty, they could smile. It sounded much easier than cleaning offices or selling cigarettes on the street. Katerina did both. And with the hostess jobs, Jakob told them, they would get a one-room apartment to live in, plus some wages to pay for other things. So for months, Katerina and Nadja had planned, waiting to hear if they'd gotten the jobs. Jakob said not to worry, it was a sure thing. But it took time to get the immigration paperwork, and they should count their blessings the company that was hiring them did all that. Most employers wouldn't.

Then the day had come when Jakob knocked on the door of Katerina's small apartment she shared with her mother.

"The paperwork is done," he'd said. "Get your things, because you need to go to the airport right away."

She'd left a note for her mother, not that it mattered. Paula Volkolva hadn't cared much about anything Katerina did in years. The older woman spent her days working as a washroom attendant at a private luncheon club before she'd move on to her other job as the second-shift housekeeper in the home of a very wealthy government official. By the time Paula came home at midnight, she didn't care where her daughter was or what she was doing. And Katerina imagined Paula wouldn't be terribly distressed she'd run off to America either. Although she'd miss Katerina's contribution to the rent.

It had all seemed so perfect those first few hours. Katerina and Nadja had been taken by bus to the airport with a group of other young women. There were twelve of them, and they waited in a special lounge at a private airstrip for a small jet they were told was owned by the company they'd be working for.

Katerina had never been to an airport, flown on a plane, or lived outside her mother's neighborhood in Moscow. She had been in awe of the sight of the jet sitting on a darkened runway when they were finally allowed to board late at night.

They'd spent the next fourteen hours flying. First to Helsinki where they boarded a different plane, and then to the city that was supposed to be their new home—Chicago, USA. She watched the sun sparkle off the mirrored windows of the skyscrapers as their plane had swung over the city on its descent. It had been morning when they'd landed, and even as exhausted as she was, Katerina had experienced a surge of hope unlike anything she'd ever felt.

Finally, she'd thought. Finally her life was going to change. She stepped off the plane, took a deep breath, and opened herself to all the possibilities she'd never allowed herself to consider. A beautiful home, a safe neighborhood, a family that loved her.

Then a large man named Sergei had grabbed her arm and muscled her into the pitch-black back of a generic van, and her entire future had crumbled like the bricks of her mother's apartment block.

**

The heavy bag thudded dully as Cian punched it—right, left. Right, left. Sweat beaded his brow, and he grunted with the exertion of each deadly blow.

"When I was a younger man, I won many amateur fights in Moscow," an accented voice said behind him. Cian pulled his last punch and turned slowly to face a stocky man who looked to be in his late forties, but still impressively fit—broad chested, hard as steel.

His gaze darted over the man's shoulder where he saw two men with obvious shoulder holsters standing alongside the door. But he also saw his own men on the catwalk that ran around the high ceiling, AR-15s aimed at the Russians, who apparently hadn't realized the competition was there.

Cian gave the man a cold smile. "I'm guessing you're not here to tell me you've moved in next door and you're bringing cookies."

The man's cold expression didn't crack. "Oh, I'm moving in next door, Mr. MacFarlane, but I'm definitely not bringing cookies." He began to stroll casually around the area, looking at the equipment, touching a weight, inspecting a bag. "My name is Sergei Petrov. I am a businessman, like yourself, and I have recently acquired the rights to operate here in Chicago."

Cian pulled off first one glove, then the other, slowly unwrapping the tape on his hands afterward. He leaned back on the nearby fighting platform, letting the ropes dig into the bare skin of his back.

"That's odd," he said with a smile. "I don't recall giving anyone permission to operate here in Chicago."

Sergei chuckled, but even that was cold as ice. "No, you wouldn't. We don't ask permission from others, merely take what we desire."

"And while that may have worked in New York…or Moscow," Cian answered as if he'd barely heard the man, "that's not how things work here."

Sergei snorted in derision. "You really think you can stop me?" he asked, stepping closer.

Cian kept his gaze firm and pushed off the ledge he leaned against, coming nose to nose with Sergei. "Oh, I know I can," he answered in a low voice. "Whatever you think you're going to be doing here, you're dead wrong. Nothing goes on in Chicago without my permission. It's MacFarlane territory, and that's not going to change."

"And the Mexicans?" Sergei asked, eyes narrowed.

"Because I allow them," Cian spat. "And they

know it as well as you do."

Sergei leaned in closer, his voice almost a whisper as he replied. "Yet, for someone who is so in control, you appear to have none at the moment. Your brothers don't have what it takes to stop me, we both know it, and your father is sick in the body and the mind. What's to keep me from simply killing you now and doing whatever the hell I want?"

Cian grinned, then gestured at the ceiling. "Go ahead," he said mildly. "Try it."

Sergei's gaze went up, and the moment he realized what waited in the rafters, his skin mottled red with fury.

"Home field advantage," Cian said with a slight tilt of his head.

Sergei began backing away, anger making his movements jerky. "We're not done, MacFarlane. The battle might have been won, but war is long, and I have lived through many."

Cian waved like a prom queen as Sergei jerked his chin at his men and marched out the doors.

"That was badass, boss," Danny said, strolling out from behind the door of the back office where he'd been skulking.

"That," Cian answered as he reached for his water bottle and took a long draught to calm his racing pulse, "was only the beginning."

**

Ever vigilant, Liam MacFarlane watched as his brother's men unloaded cargo from a truck outside a warehouse his family owned along the I-90. He stood, legs slightly spread, hands hanging loosely in front of him, a Ruger 9mm tucked in the holster under his arm, which he made no effort to conceal.

"Mr. Mac," one of the guys called as he held a box labeled *Bath Salts*, "Do you want all these to go in the warehouse, or should we leave some in the truck?"

"It all goes here," he answered. The forty-seven boxes would be here for only a few hours while the "bath salts" were repacked into smaller boxes with shipping labels that would send them all over the country. First thing tomorrow morning, the United States Postal Service would be collecting the new packages and distributing them like it did for a million other businesses all over the country every day.

The only difference being these boxes were filled with opioids and heroin.

The idea had been cooked up between his younger brother Finn and Xavier Rossi, the sleazy hacker who originally ran the dark website Rogue. It was simple, really—place drugs in with lavender bath salts to help disguise the appearance and odor, take orders on the website, then ship the product via good old-fashioned US Mail.

Liam had to admit, it had sounded like a whole lot of stupid when he'd first heard the plan, but business had been booming for two months now, with no signs of stopping, and the postal service had no clue what they were sending around the country. But really, he thought, why had he ever doubted? Finn had planned it out, and Finn was a freakin' genius.

Liam's phone chimed, and he looked at the screen, seeing a text from Cian.

You done with the shipment yet?

He texted back, his big thumbs less than agile on the smooth screen. As Finn often said, he needed to get a "Liam-sized" phone.

Just about. You need me?

He watched as the dots danced across the screen. His heart took an extra beat or two as it always did when he worried about Cian. After all, Cian was his best friend, the guy he'd looked up to his entire life, the reason he did what he did and was who he was.

Meet me at Banshee when you're done. We need to talk.

Dammit. Liam looked impatiently at his phone. Everything had been a clusterfuck for the last two months. His youngest brother, Connor, had made a series of immature mistakes that had nearly gotten the family into a war with their nearest rivals, then he'd left the family and the business altogether, a decision Liam was still unsure about but had agreed to support because Cian asked him to.

As if all that wasn't enough, they now had Russians on their asses, looking to expand territory, and Cian had somehow gotten tangled up in the management of Rogue when Xavier made an untimely exit from this world. Well, it hadn't actually *somehow* happened—his brother had a hard-on for Rogue's genius second-in-command, Lila Rodriguez.

Yeah, any calls from his brothers these days probably meant some new nightmare.

"Let's get a move on," he directed his men as he crossed his arms and kept his gaze scanning the tarmac behind the warehouse they were using. "I need to get back to the office."

His guys picked up the pace, and a few minutes later, everything was unloaded and ready to be repackaged. Liam left instructions for the guards who would stay with the product until his brother Finn's crew got there and readied everything for pickup by the USPS. Keeping the product on the move was a hassle but had served them well—most of the time.

As he rode in the Cadillac Escalade driven by his second, Jimmy Flanigan, he texted Finn.

Shipment's ready.

Finn replied in a hot second. *Great. Sending crew over now. You on the way to Banshee?*

Yeah. Know what's up?

Nope, but I got the call too.

Great, Liam thought. It was something bad. *Fuck.*

When they pulled into the back parking lot at Banshee, Liam told Jimmy he was free to grab a drink at the bar while the MacFarlane brothers met. Cian's guard, Danny, was standing outside Cian's office door as Liam entered the building, the big metal door to the parking lot closing behind him with a clang. He paused for a moment to let his eyes adjust to the dusky light in the small hallway.

"Hey, boss," Danny said casually.

"How's everything going today?" Liam asked. As the family's enforcer, he oversaw all security. So while each of his brothers had personal guards, those men were ultimately Liam's responsibility, and it was one he took seriously.

"We had a little run-in, but everyone's fine. I'm sure that's what you're here to talk about," Danny answered, twisting the doorknob and sweeping his arm out for Liam to enter.

Liam stalked into the office to find Cian leaning his ass against the edge of the desk while he talked on the phone.

"I'm glad she's not too sick. I'm sending another

guy over so one can stay at her room and the other can be with you at all times... I know, it's not forever," Cian said softly, his gaze on Liam. "Liam's here. Can we agree to it for now, and I'll be over as soon as possible?"

Liam's skin felt slightly itchy like it did whenever he heard that tone in his brother's voice. He was talking to Lila, and Liam hadn't decided if Lila was okay for Cian yet. It was obvious Cian had a real thing for the pretty hacker, but Liam couldn't see anything good coming out of the deal. He loved all his brothers, but it was Cian he owed his very existence to, and he'd made it his life's work to repay that debt.

That meant saving Cian from his own misguided inclinations if necessary. So far, Liam thought Lila was exactly that, a misguided inclination.

Cian murmured something else to Lila that Liam decided not to hear, then hung up.

"You see Finn coming?" Cian asked, moving around the desk to sit in the big pleather desk chair.

"No, but he texted. Should be here any minute."

Cian nodded and leaned back, running a hand through his stylish, perfect hair. Two years older but an inch shorter than Liam, and lean, Cian was all male model while Liam was more heavyweight fighter—muscles that bulged, tattoos that crept out of sleeves and collars. And while Cian had the cover-boy hair, Liam's was buzz cut—simple, easy to maintain, and part of the package he'd honed carefully over the years since he was sixteen.

Liam was what Finn had once termed "a quintessential badass," and for anyone who questioned why he'd chosen that, he'd tell them how well it served him when he'd been incarcerated for three months at the age of twenty-nine. They'd put his father in a separate facility when the two of them were arrested while taking possession of a shipment of heroin. Fucking FBI thought if they split them up, they'd make one of them flip.

But even without his father's influence to protect him, Liam had made it through his incarceration intact—in every sense of the word. And that was because he was over six feet of hard, honed, no-nonsense warrior. His only regret about being inside was he'd had to leave Cian alone, but he'd kept tabs from prison and done everything he could to ensure his older brother was safe.

The door opened, and Finn slid in like a kid trying to beat the tardy bell into class.

"What's up?" he asked as he looked from Cian to Liam and back again.

"Sit," Cian commanded. Both younger brothers dropped into chairs like obedient puppies. "Lila—or I should say *Xavier*—was contacted by the Russians this morning."

The late head of Rogue, Xavier had been secretly working with the Russians to destroy the MacFarlanes, and when Lila had discovered it and confronted him, he'd attacked her. She'd killed him in self-defense.

"So they haven't figured out he's dead yet?"

"They obviously suspect something. It was time for his monthly payoff, and he hasn't been communicating with them, so they were getting pissy."

"What did you tell her to do about it?" Finn asked, his floppy brown hair hanging over one emerald-green eye.

Cian leaned forward, putting his forearms on the desktop, his Henley sleeves shoved up to his elbows.

Cian said, "She answered them, gave them some information I fed her, and the money showed up in Xavier's off-shore account like it has every other month."

Liam watched Cian closely. "But that's not the whole story, is it?"

Cian gave him a wry grin. "Busted."

"What the fuck did you do?" Liam asked, his blood pressure spiking because he could tell his brother had taken an unnecessary risk.

"The info we fed them involved me being unprotected at the gym."

All the MacFarlane brothers worked out at O'Neil's boxing gym, and the owner, Sean O'Neil, was an old friend of the family and the father of Connor's girlfriend, Jess.

Liam clenched his fists. "Please tell me you didn't use yourself as bait for the Russians."

"Okay," Cian said, shrugging lightly, his expression guilty.

"Jesus Christ," Liam spat. "What the hell is the matter with you? And Danny let you do that shit? He's fucking fired."

Finn smirked, and Liam resisted the urge to slug him in the arm the way he would have when they were children.

"He has to do what I tell him. You know that as well as I do," Cian answered calmly. How the hell he could be so calm when he'd risked his damn life a few hours ago, Liam didn't know.

Liam took a deep breath and slowly let it out through his nose. "What happened?"

"They showed," Cian answered. "Of course, I wasn't actually alone, so everybody's in one piece, but I don't think *Sergei* and I are ever going to be besties."

"You met them, then?" Finn asked.

"That's one way of putting it," Cian answered, his eyes narrowing. "And now that we have a name, Lila's finding out everything she can about him. It appears he's one of their top earners. He's been the number two guy in Brooklyn for the last few years, and Chicago's all his if he can get us out of the way."

"Like to see him try," Liam snarled.

"We need a strategy for dealing with this," Cian said bluntly, looking at Finn.

Finn was the family fixer—he fixed crime scenes as well as issues that required diplomacy. Liam appreciated Finn's skills, but he didn't always agree they were the best approach.

"Let me handle them," he growled, itching to bash some heads. "We'll find out where they're holing up and come up with a plan. Hit them hard once, it'll be over in a few hours."

Cian looked like he was considering it, but then shook his head slightly. "It's tempting, but then we bring the New York organization down on us. I honestly don't think we have the manpower to go to war with them."

Liam sighed and leaned back in his seat, trying to control the adrenaline spike he always got when there was a chance of war. He never told Cian how much he needed it—the violence. He knew it wasn't healthy, but he got a certain kind of satisfaction when he could control an outcome with nothing more than his body and a piece of metal in his hand. He'd felt completely out of control only once in his life—when he was a sixteen-year old boy with a gun pointed at his head—and he'd vowed right then and there, he'd never feel like that again.

"From what I know about the Russians, trying to negotiate is pointless," Finn said. "They're not like anything we're used to. They don't care about family, so you can't get leverage on them that way. They don't give a damn if you slaughter half their soldiers either, as long as they win in the end."

Cian shoved at a file folder on his desk, sending the papers inside spilling out across the scarred wood. "Well, that's just dandy. What the hell are we supposed to do, then?"

"Attack a different way," Finn said calmly.

"And that would mean?" Liam asked.

"We look for a way to feed them to the cops. If we can get the Russians investigated, it'll distract them from our turf."

"So like, phone in anonymous tips or something?" Liam asked, trying to picture how something like that would play out.

"Mm." Finn pursed his lips in thought. "I'm thinking maybe we send one of us to turn informant."

"Hell no!" Liam leaped to his feet. "Are you crazy?"

His gaze shot to Cian, who looked suddenly pale, and with good reason. Playing with the feds was an invitation to put all of them in prison.

"Just hear me out," Finn said. Cian nodded and gave Liam a look that had "sit down" written all over it. Liam couldn't, but he did lean against the adjacent wall, arms crossed over his thick chest.

"We have Lila work her magic on the Russians— their offshore accounts, their personnel, their various activities—then we make contact with the law, tell them we have info for them, and the trade is they'll get the Russians off our backs."

Cian scowled. "Too dangerous," he said. "Our snitch says one wrong thing and they could bring the feds down on all of us in a flash. There's a reason we don't play with the law."

"We can coach them, keep a mic on them so we can hear what they say, even have them wear an earpiece," Finn argued.

"Look, we have a great bunch of soldiers, but I'm not willing to risk putting one of them into a situation where the feds might try to take advantage. They'll use the opportunity to pressure our guy, and while I don't doubt their loyalty, normally, I'm not willing to chance them flipping on us if they're faced with that kind of pressure."

"Liam's right," Cian said. "There's no one we could trust to that extent."

"There's me," Finn said defiantly.

Liam cursed softly, glaring at Finn. The blood rushed in his ears for a moment as his heart rate soared as if he'd just boxed a round.

Cian stared at Finn, speechless for once.

"Hear me out," Finn said. "Lila does our research for us, I take it to the CPD, not the Feds. We'll look at options for who to contact before we make a move—choose a detective in the CPD who has the right demographics. Someone who's new, doesn't know all the ins and outs of having a CI, someone who's not known for being a hard-ass but wants a chance to make a name, get a promotion."

"And what if someone finds out you're talking to the cops?" Liam asked. "You could end up dead, because while everyone in this room knows you'd never betray us, there are plenty of people who don't."

"Pop being one," Cian muttered.

"Oh hell," Liam agreed. "He could never find out." He gave Cian a long, hard look. They both knew something Finn and their youngest brother Connor had been spared, and it meant one thing—get in Robbie MacFarlane's way and you could very well end up dead, even if you were his own flesh and blood.

"He wouldn't find out," Finn said assuredly. "I'd only meet with the cop a couple of times. Dump the info, then disappear. I lay low for a few weeks, they get busy screwing with the Russians, life goes back to normal."

Cian sighed as he stood. "I don't like it."

Liam concurred. "I hate it."

"Think about it, at least," Finn said. Cian reluctantly said he'd think on it, and they all moved to exit the office.

As he walked back down the hall to the parking lot, all Liam could think was there was no way he was going to let his younger brother get tangled with the law. He'd survived prison. Finn wouldn't. It was time to take things into his own hands. Even if it meant disobeying the man he'd sworn to serve for the rest of his life.

Chapter Three

"I'll be right back, Mom," Lila said softly to the frail woman in the hospital bed.

"Mm," her mother murmured without even opening her eyes. The surgery had gone well, but her mother's body was wrecked by weeks of chemotherapy, and Lila still had a nauseous ache in her gut when she looked at the only family member she had left.

She stuffed her phone in the back pocket of her jeans and quietly slipped out the door of the room.

In the hallway were two mobsters, one glued to the door of her mother's room, the other leaning against the wall opposite, his eyes sharp as he watched her walk toward him.

"Cian just texted. He's waiting for me in the lounge at the end of the hall."

Louis nodded. "Yep, I'll walk you down there and wait outside while you talk."

Lila gave him a weak smile before they started

down the hall. The hum of the hospital had become so familiar in the last six weeks, Lila didn't notice it much at this point.

When they reached the lounge, she said hello to Cian's personal guard, Danny, then took a deep breath before opening the door. Cian was looking at his phone, his back to the door, the fading light from the window in front of him creating a halo around his form, throwing Lila's heart into a stuttering rhythm she hated.

Six weeks ago, she'd spent her first night in the man's arms, fully expecting to be on a private jet to an island somewhere the next day—but instead, she'd gotten the news her mother had brain cancer. An only child, Lila had done what responsible daughters do and put her escape plans on ice to take care of her mother while also running Rogue.

And ever since, she and Cian had been dancing around one another—sleeping together sporadically, pretending to be only work colleagues the remainder of the time. And she never knew which way it would be.

Cian turned as the door closed behind her, and her damn heart stuttered again.

He was a stunning man, with the face of an angel, blue eyes, black hair, sharp cheekbones. And unfortunately, she knew that beneath the black jeans and perfectly fitted blue Henley, the rest of him was just as spectacular.

"Hey," he said softly when he saw her.

"Hi." She swallowed uncomfortably.

"How's she doing?" He took a step toward her.

She shrugged. "As well as can be expected, I guess."

He stopped, his brow furrowing. She knew she was being cold, but then she needed to be if she was ever going to get out of this mess.

Cian cleared his throat. "I'm sorry you're having to deal with the Russians in the middle of all this."

"S'okay," she answered, sounding somewhat defeated.

He reached out and put a finger under her chin, bringing her gaze to his. "What's going on?" he asked gently.

She stared at him, and she couldn't answer. She…just…

"Hey." He pulled her into him, wrapping his arms around her as he held her against his warm chest. His mouth brushed along the hair near her ear. "Tell me what you need. Anything. More help for your mom? More staff at Rogue?"

What did it say when the first thing that popped into her head was: *You. I need you?* Being held by him was the first time in days she'd felt safe or whole or like she wasn't on the verge of losing everything.

But he wasn't an option, and spending time near him was always dangerous. Hence all the big men waiting in the hallway.

"Lila?" he asked again.

She tried not to linger, breathing in his scent— pine, heat, and man. "I'm sorry." She pulled away. "You're doing plenty already. I'm just worn out. Once I have a good night's sleep, I'll be fine."

As she walked toward the windows, looking out at the small courtyard that lay between the two wings of the hospital, she sensed his presence behind her. She heard his exhale and felt his heat. Then his hands were on her shoulders, and he was turning her toward him.

"You know I didn't think you'd still be here six weeks later," he said, his voice a low rumble.

"I know," she answered sadly. She hadn't expected it either. If she had, she would never have climbed in his bed in the first place. Because she'd known the first time he'd touched her, she'd never be able to say no if he were near. The only way to expunge Cian MacFarlane from her life was to be on the other side of the world from him.

His hands moved from her shoulders to her neck, his fingers wrapping around her nape and pulling her closer, inch by painfully erotic inch.

As his lips descended until they were only inches from hers, her heart nearly beat out of her chest.

"I haven't been able to forget a single second with you," he whispered. "Even though I know we shouldn't do this anymore, I can't stop thinking about it."

She blinked, then sighed softly, her resistance waning, just as it had several other times in the last few weeks. But by now, she knew the dance—he'd press, she'd relent, they'd fall into the nearest bed, then both realize they never should have mixed sex with business and go back to being colleagues, back to the unrequited longing.

"You were supposed to leave, Lila from Rogue," he murmured, his eyes scanning her face.

"Sorry?" she squeaked, her palm landing on his chest and digging in despite her efforts to stay unaffected.

"I wanted you safe. I still do, but now I also just want you." He leaned down and brushed his lips over hers. "Night." Again. "And." Again. "Day."

The room was silent then, as they drank each other in, first in sips, then in gulps, like oxygen they couldn't live without. His hands roamed over her, touching, squeezing, caressing. And all her normally rational thoughts scattered like a flock of birds in a park. She melted into him, gambling once more, tangling her fingers in his hair, tasting him as he became more important than anything else in her world.

Then a buzzing sound broke through the haze of want, and Cian cursed as he pulled away. She reluctantly released him, and he reached into his front pocket, retrieving his phone. He looked at it, and his jaw tensed before his thumbs flew over the keyboard for a moment, then he shoved the phone back in his pocket and turned to her.

"I have to…" He gestured toward the door.

"Yeah, it's fine. I should get back to my mom." She moved to step around him, but he caught her upper arm in his big hand.

"Lila?" He leaned down, his lips nearly skimming her cheek. "I came here to talk about what needs to happen next with the Russians. They're going to know I'm onto their arrangement with you—with Xavier."

"Okay. You know how to find me." She nearly laughed at that one. With his bodyguards protecting her, it was more like she was his prisoner than anything else.

"You didn't let me finish," he said. "I came here to talk business, but I think it's past time we talked about other things." One of his eyebrows lifted, and Lila dug her teeth into her lower lip.

"What other things?"

"This," he said, pointing between them. "I didn't think you'd be here after this long, but you are, and whether it's for six more days or six more months, we need to talk about it."

"You don't have to, really. It's fine, I get that we can't—"

"Maybe we can," he said huskily. "Maybe I've decided we need to. Let me see you next week—after your mom's doing better. We'll get some food ordered in at my place. We'll talk. About all of it. The Russians. Xavier. *Us.*"

She knew she shouldn't. It would only give her hope where there wasn't any. Give her ideas where there were already too many. She sighed.

"Lila from Rogue," he murmured, tucking a piece of her dark hair behind her ear.

"Okay."

He grinned then. "I'll have the boys bring you by at seven on Tuesday."

Then he was gone, striding out the door and on to the next dangerous, insane thing in his dangerous, insane life.

Dammit, Lila thought as her heart ached. How could she be so smart and so stupid all at the same time?

**

"You sure you want to do this?" Finn's voice came through Liam's earpiece as he stood in the dark, leaning against the old brick wall of an empty slaughterhouse.

"Yeah. I need to know what they have going on in there."

He watched the nondescript metal door across the street as two big men with slicked-back hair and cheap clothes exited and climbed into a dark Escalade before pulling away from the curb.

"You really ought to have someone with you, Liam," Finn reprimanded. "You'd never allow Cian to do something like this. And he'd kick both our asses if he knew you were doing it."

Liam watched the door for another moment, something pulling at him to get over there and find out what the Russians were hiding.

"Yeah, what Cian doesn't know won't hurt him, and I'm going to be in and out in fifteen. You can start timing me right about...now." He disconnected the call and casually strolled across the street, watching the front of the old factory as he went. The windows on the bottom level were all blacked out, while the top floors were simply dark. It was impossible to tell if anyone was inside or not.

He walked along past the building, never breaking stride until he reached the corner where he turned, scanning the area to see if anyone was noticing him. There were very few cars around and no other pedestrians, so he felt pretty secure.

It had taken a fair amount of head bashing to get the location of the Russians' hideout in town. He'd had his men running down leads for several days, but he'd found the place, and then he'd spent many more hours watching, waiting, logging the patterns of activity. The place was pretty much dead until around ten p.m. at night. There was a woman who came in late morning and left late afternoon. She had cleaning supplies and groceries with her, so she appeared to be some sort of housekeeper. The rest of the time, it was limited to changing security.

And between seven p.m. and ten p.m., the activity was at its absolute lowest. The guards he'd just seen would leave, and by his count, there was only one guy left inside. At ten, bouncers would show up and then customers. He wasn't sure what they were selling inside, but he had a bad feeling it might be more than drugs, because customers were inside for a lot longer than a drug buy took.

When he hit the alley that ran behind the building, he quickly moved along the back wall until he reached the fire escape. He jumped up and grabbed the metal railing of the staircase and hoisted himself up onto the first landing, being remarkably quiet considering his size. Then it was up the steep stairs to the second floor, where he'd discovered a window slightly ajar the day before.

He breathed a sigh of relief to find it still not locked. But it was jammed, and it took him nearly five minutes to wedge it open far enough he could shimmy through. Liam wasn't generally the kind of guy who shimmied, but desperate times and all. The room he entered was dark and smelled of mold and damp. He tiptoed through, finding the exit locked.

"Fuck," he muttered as he reached into the pocket of his leather jacket and produced a small lockpick kit. After a few moments to find the right-size tool, he felt the dead bolt begin to slide, and the door made a quiet click as the bolt retreated.

Liam listened for a moment, hearing nothing, before he opened the door and slipped out into the hallway.

The hall was only dimly lit and empty. Out here, the flooring was new and the walls freshly painted.

The smell of lumber told him there had been some construction done recently as well.

He walked along, gun drawn, listening for any sign of life. When he finally reached another door, he stopped and pressed his ear to it. At first, he thought there was nothing, but then he heard a slight thump followed by a muffled voice. He couldn't make out the words, but it definitely sounded like a woman.

He waited, listening—another thump, more of the same voice. He closed his eyes and let his instincts take over. Since he was sixteen, Liam had spent his life honing his body and his instincts. He was a warrior in every sense of the word, and if he didn't trust himself, he couldn't do his job, and he especially couldn't be as damn good at it as he was.

Instinct kicked in, and he made the decision—stepping back, he lifted his leg and planted his boot along the edge of the door as hard as he could. The wood splintered away from the frame and swung open, slamming into the wall inside the little room, revealing a disheveled woman duct-taped to a chair.

Liam stepped through, expecting her to start screaming, although it wouldn't have mattered much since her mouth was taped shut as well. But instead of panicking, she narrowed her eyes and tried to say something behind her tape prison. By the look on her face, it wasn't anything nice.

He quietly shut the door behind him and moved toward her. She growled. Actually growled, and he paused, taking her in. She had long blonde hair, lank and wavy. Her eyes looked like a raccoon's, with heavy makeup smeared around them. Her throat and chest were covered in bruises, some older, some newer, all ugly in spite of her beauty.

As his gaze traveled lower, he got a jolt south of the waistband when he saw she was wearing nothing but lingerie of some sort, the satin and lace covering nothing more than the essentials. He couldn't help the grin that broke out across his face. She was absolutely his type—blonde, busty and bare.

"Well, hello there," he said, one eyebrow raised.

She struggled against her restraints, looking like she wanted to take a chunk out of him.

"Shh, shh," he soothed as he knelt next to her. "Here's how this will work—I'm not going to hurt you unless you force me to. I'll take that tape off your mouth if you tell me what the Russians are doing here. I'll take your bonds off if you tell me a few names, and I'll get you out of here if you give me information beyond names. Like how many of these guys there are." He paused and reached to push a strand of her hair out of her face. She growled again, but it wasn't as aggressive, more wary.

"Do we have a deal?" he asked.

She looked at him, considering, then nodded slowly.

He gave her a quick grimace. "I'm sorry, but the only way to do this is fast and hard." Her eyes widened in fear as he grabbed the end of the duct tape across her mouth and yanked it off in one smooth motion.

She kept her mouth closed and made a long sound of frustration. Where the tape had been, her porcelain skin was red and splotchy, but already, Liam could see more of her, and it was exquisite—high cheekbones, full lips, a perfectly proportioned nose. He tried not to stare and to keep his mind on the fact that time was ticking down and someone could come for this woman at any point.

"Okay, what is this place?"

She was breathing hard and her eyes were glossy with unshed tears, but her voice was a complete surprise. First, because it was raspy like a torch singer's, and second, because her accent was Russian.

"It is hell," she spat in answer to his question.

"Maybe, but I want to know what they're doing here."

"And who are you?" she asked. "*Politsiya*?"

He laughed bitterly. "No, babe, I'm about as far from the police as you can get. Now, what are they doing here?"

"Selling things," she said bitterly.

"Drugs?"

She shrugged, the movement distracting him as her braless breasts jiggled with the motion.

"Probably."

"And?" he prompted, nearing the end of his patience.

Her face paled, and she stiffened as she answered.

"People," she finally ground out.

Fuck. Liam's heart sank. His family had spent a few decades doing illegal things—gambling, smuggling, drugs—but they'd never once trafficked in human beings, and God help him, with Cian at the helm, Liam didn't have to worry they ever would.

"So they're bringing girls from Russia?" He moved behind her to tear the duct tape off her wrists. After her arms had been released, they hung by her sides as her voice wavered for a moment. It must hurt like hell, all that blood rushing back into her hands, but she didn't break.

"Yes. They tell us we come to US for jobs. We fly on airplane, then when we arrive, they put us in a van and bring us here."

He went to her front and began to work on the bonds that held her ankles to the chair legs.

"Who's in charge, Petrov?"

"Sergei, yes," she answered. "I don't know how many other men, but there is one called Micael and one called Alexei."

"Where are the other girls? How many?"

"Twelve. They keep us in one room downstairs. Then at night, they take us out—a few at a time." Her jaw turned to iron, and her eyes got a faraway look. Liam swallowed, fully understanding what she wasn't saying as well as what she was.

He took his jacket off and held it out. "Here. It'll cover you until we can get you someplace safe."

She reached out to take it, then stopped. "What about the others?"

His gaze snapped to his Apple watch—only about two minutes left until Finn called in the cavalry and started a war. "Babe, our time is running out. I'm sorry for the other girls, but I can't take on the Bratva alone. We'll get you out and then…" He shrugged, because he wasn't going to promise he'd rescue eleven other women forced into sexual slavery. He wasn't sure he was that good a guy.

She shook her head stubbornly, and he got a sinking feeling.

"No. I only go with my friend."

Shit.

"Where is she?" he asked, even as he knew he wasn't going to be able to take them both.

"Downstairs with the others."

God, he'd never had much desire to be a hero, but right about now, Liam wished he could make this woman's wishes come true.

"I'm sorry," he said sympathetically.

She took a deep breath and then sat back down on the chair. "It's okay. I will help myself. It is stupid to think man will do it for me."

"Your choice," he tossed off, even though he felt a sharp pang of guilt for leaving her here.

She just looked at him coldly.

He moved toward the door, sliding back into his jacket, but before he opened it, he twisted and looked at her over his shoulder. "Two more questions." She didn't respond, just kept staring at him blindly.

"What's your name?"

"Katerina," she said quietly. "Katya."

He rolled it over on his tongue as he asked the next question. "Katya...what did you do to get put in here?"

She smiled, but it was grim. "I bit off the cock of the man who paid for me," she answered.

Chapter Four

"You did *what?*"

Liam watched as Cian paced the floor of his penthouse.

"Told you," Finn muttered.

"And *you* let him?" Cian stabbed an accusing finger at Finn.

"In case you haven't noticed, I don't really have a lot of control over him," Finn shot back, waving to Liam's greater height and muscle mass.

"You should have alerted *me!*" Cian stopped in front of Finn and gestured like a wild man. "Hey, Cian, guess what? Liam is about to risk his life and a war with the Russians. I'm thinking maybe you should stop him."

Liam snorted. As much as he loved his brother, in their world, the man was virtually a pacifist. Always looking for the safest alternative, the negotiation or compromise or back door. He admired it about Cian, honored it, and in fact had spent his life since adulthood protecting it, taking on the role of family enforcer so Cian would be spared. But it didn't mean Cian was always right. Sometimes you had to take a risk, make a stand, do something that wasn't the safe choice but would get results.

And dammit, he'd gotten results. They now knew exactly what the Russians were up to and where. As sickening as it was.

"What's done is done," he told Cian as he moved from his perch against the wall and sank into the leather sofa. "Let's focus on what matters—the fact the Russians have started sex trafficking in our territory."

"Tell me again about this girl you found?" Cian asked, arms crossed as he walked to the big windows that overlooked the Chicago skyline.

"She was Russian, but she spoke English well enough to get by. She said they'd lied to her and some friend, told them they'd have legit jobs, then when they got 'em here, locked them up and started bringing in the clients."

"Damn," Finn murmured. "It's a hard world, but that's harder than normal."

"It's sick is what it is. If a woman chooses to sell herself, that's her business, but there's no place for slavery in my town. *Ever.*" Cian's tone was serious, and in spite of the pacifist tendencies, Liam knew his brother wasn't a man to make empty threats.

"And this girl you found—she wouldn't leave her friend? That's why you walked away?" Finn asked.

Liam's throat tightened, and his adrenaline kicked up a notch. It wasn't as if he didn't feel guilty. Of course he did, but what the hell was he supposed to do? Drag her kicking and screaming out of the place?

Well, actually, on the ride home, he'd realized that was exactly what he should have done. Slapped the tape back over her mouth, thrown her over his shoulder, and booked it. It was what Cian would have done. Or Finn. Cian because he wouldn't be able to leave a woman in distress. Finn because his big brain would have realized she had more information that could be useful to them. It had taken Liam nearly half an hour afterward to puzzle that one out.

"Yeah," he answered. "But I know I should have taken her anyway. Leaving her was a dumbass thing to do. She could have told us all kinds of useful info if we'd had time to question her. I only discovered what you can get from a terrified chick in five minutes flat." He looked up at Cian, who was still pondering the skyline outside. "I fucked up."

"You got out in one piece." Cian turned around and looked at Liam fiercely. "That's all that matters— ever. I feel for the woman, but as long as you're in one piece, it was a success." Then he pointed that finger again, this time at Liam. "But that doesn't mean you should have done it."

"Moving on," Finn interrupted. Liam sighed in relief. Cian could lecture for hours. "What's our next step here. The Russians are settling in, and people are going to realize it before long. It'll erode our power base, make us look weak if we don't do something. I assume you're not going to let me go to the cops with the address Liam found out and info about a slave house?"

Cian began pacing again. "No. I appreciate the offer, but I don't want any of us near the cops, that's not an option. And it's not going to do us any good to go up against them gun to gun. They're a bottomless well of resources—an international organization."

"*We're* an international organization," Liam retorted. "When was the last time you or Pop called on Dublin to help us out?" He raised an eyebrow at his brothers. "That would be never. And why the hell not? The Mexicans have friends south of the border in the cartels. The Russians have friends in Moscow and at banks all over the world. Why don't we take advantage of our relations in Ireland? They've never hesitated to have us take their men when they get into scrapes over there. Hell, half our upper-level guys are hiding out from shit that went down in Dublin or Belfast."

"Giving out visas and jobs is hardly the same as asking Dublin for guns, money, and soldiers," Cian corrected. "We need a smarter way to beat them."

"We need to do to them what the Russians have been doing to the US for the last two years," Finn said. "We need a cyberwar."

Liam watched Cian's face as he considered Finn's suggestion. "Explain what that would look like," Cian demanded, finally taking a seat on the edge of a big leather armchair.

"We're in a unique position right now. The perfect position to deal with the Russians. Like I said the other day, we have access to Lila and to everything at Rogue. We can attack them in entirely different ways than with guns and men."

It was as though Liam could see the invisible ideas bouncing through the air between his brothers. Sometimes he hated that he wasn't always as clear on what was coming as they seemed to be.

"Target their bank accounts?" Cian asked.

"For starters. Hack their phones, disrupt their internet, hide their money, screw with the electricity at their brothel. Basically be the housefly they can't get rid of."

"And eventually, you think they'll come to us asking to negotiate a peace?"

Finn shrugged. "I think it'll get some sort of reaction from them that'll tell you what to do next."

"And if the reaction is that they come into one of our clubs or warehouses firing AKs?" Liam asked. Because it was what he would do if he were the Russians and a *housefly* like the Dublin Devils was interfering with business.

"They won't react that way," Finn said confidently. "More likely they'll go after our financials and records as well. But they don't have Lila. She's an international rock star in the hacking world. It'll be a hell of a lot harder to get to us that way than they'd ever guess."

Cian stood. "I'm not agreeing to anything yet, but I'll talk to Lila about it. But in the meantime, no more visits to the brothel." He pinned Liam with a glare.

Liam put his hands up, palms out. But he didn't promise anything. Somewhere deep inside, he knew he might not keep the promise if it were made.

Because somewhere deep inside, Liam knew he'd have to go back for the girl Katya…and her friend.

**

In the quiet of the night, Lila sat in her small living room, three computer screens surrounding her as she tapped rapidly at a keyboard. She muttered to herself, reading bits and pieces of information that flew across the screens. On one, she had a list of Rogue personnel—the wizards who created the dark website, and the technicians who used it—on the third, she had the history of Xavier Rossi's communications with the Russians, and on the middle display, she had one of seven bank accounts belonging to Robbie MacFarlane and housed in the Cayman Islands.

She tapped out a group communication to the Rogue staff, telling them to switch out all security codes at precisely five a.m. Central US time the next day. She debated for a moment, then signed it with her own name. She'd begun running Rogue after Xavier's untimely death, and those first few weeks, she'd impersonated him, but slowly, one by one, those staff who seemed determined to speak directly to Xavier had either quit or been fired when they pressed too hard on the issue. Almost all of those who remained seemed not to care whether their orders came from Xavier or Lila or a piece of cheddar cheese, as long as the instructions were clear and the paycheck arrived on time.

After she sent the message to her staff—she still got a little giddy rush every time she thought of them that way, *her* staff—she bounced back over to the Cayman bank accounts. There was one in particular that caught her attention because it had never had a withdrawal, but deposits came regularly. She began the tedious process of cracking the encryption for the account, stopping only to take sips of the green tea she kept on hand when she worked late. And since taking over Rogue, Lila worked late nearly every night.

Forty minutes later, she finally got into the account. She began to scroll through the history, seeing nothing but a long string of deposits which she discovered had been regular and ongoing for more than two decades. Every five years or so, the amount would jump incrementally higher, but the deposits never ceased, not once in all those years, and the amount was now up to one hundred thousand dollars each time. The source, she saw as she looked more carefully, was the Bank of Ireland.

She examined the account number the deposit originated from. If Irish accounts followed the pattern of other European banks, it was a business account, not a personal one. She sighed, fatigue finally catching up to her. *Tomorrow,* she told herself. Tomorrow, she'd dig into the Irish account. But for now, she'd be glad there was nothing new on the last screen, the one that showed Xavier's communications with the Russians. Since she'd relayed the information about Cian being alone at the gym, she hadn't heard a peep. And maybe she never would again.

"Wishful thinking, Lila," she muttered, as she stretched and thought about how good the idea of going to bed sounded. The Russians would be back, but for tonight, she'd be grateful they were quiet. She pushed back her rolling chair, preparing to get on that great idea of sleeping in her comfortable bed, but then a chime sounded from screen number one. Her gaze shifted to the left.

Server C, the message read, *Code Yellow.* Lila took a deep breath, banishing thoughts of thousand-thread-count sheets and pillow-top mattresses. She clicked on the message and began to respond. Sleep wasn't coming anytime soon. Lila was too important in too many ways for that sweet relief.

**

"Your brother's been gone for weeks," Don said as he leaned against the trunk of a dark late-model sedan provided by his employer.

"So he has," Cian answered, hands on his hips as he stared at the lights of the adjacent airstrip. Cian's heart soared almost as high as the private jet taking off when he thought about Connor in the new life they'd obtained for him.

"And *so* we need to move this along," Don snapped. "I'm not getting any younger here, and I've played fair with you, Cian. I want the final piece, the piece that will not only put your father and brothers behind bars but also end the Devils for good."

Cian's blood turned cold. It didn't matter how many times they said it, when the words "brothers" and "prison" were spoken in the same sentence, it always stole a piece of his soul.

"How about something even more fun?" he asked, propping his foot on the bumper of Don's ugly-ass car and reaching for his untied bootlace. No matter what was going on inside, he'd die before he let Don see it. His movements were spare, casual, relaxed.

Finn's original idea for handling the Russian problem had been a good one, but he didn't know that Cian was already informing as the feds dug for information to shut down his family's organization. And while Cian didn't give a damn if the business went under, he cared immensely if his brothers ended up dead or in prison.

"Don't do this," Don warned. "We had a deal, and if you don't honor it I'll just take you in right now. I have plenty to put you away for a few years, and with you gone, management of the family will go to Liam. We both know he's not smart enough to stay alive."

Cian finished retying his bootlace, then propped an elbow on his bent knee. What he really wanted to do was send his fist into Don's pasty face for disparaging Liam's competence yet again. Liam wasn't like Cian and Finn. He wasn't even like Connor. He approached things differently, but the idea that Liam wasn't a survivor was very wrong and very shortsighted.

"You could," he answered. "You're forgetting Liam would still have Finn as backup, but be that as it may, you'd be missing out on something bigger than my family's business. Big Apple big. You'll be a superstar with what I have to tell you."

Don tried to look bored, but Cian could sense the man's hunger for a score. Something big enough to get him the dreamed-of promotion he was angling after.

Don shrugged in nonchalant agreement.

"Bratva," Cian said, letting the word hang in the night air around them as another plane taxied down the adjacent runway, its engines roaring, the smell of jet fuel permeating the air around them.

"Continue, but this doesn't mean you won't still owe me the info on your family."

Cian ignored the warning.

"They've decided they want to take over Chicago, and they've set up a slave shop."

"Fuck." Don's jaw tensed.

"Yeah," Cian concurred. "From what we know, they're bringing in girls from Russia, warehousing them at a place over on East Twenty-Third."

"Goddamn Russians. They keep getting guys inside ICE. I've heard of at least four other times in the last six months, they've slipped women into the country illegally in Denver and New York."

"But now you know exactly where they are. Do what you do and bust 'em, Officer." Cian grinned obnoxiously at the fed.

Don's lip curled before his phone chimed, and he pulled it from his pocket, looking at it quickly.

"I have to go. This conversation isn't over," he warned, pointing a finger at Cian.

Cian knew it wasn't, but he was damn happy to be done with it for now.

"I'll be in touch, and I'll want all the information you have on them," Don said, striding to the driver's side of the car.

Yeah, Cian thought, *the Russians ought to keep Don and company busy and out of the way for a while.* Even Cian knew he was running out of things to distract the FBI with, though, and that meant his brothers were in greater danger every day.

He still had his biggest ace in the hole—Rogue. The dark website's business would be solid gold to the feds. The only problem? Lila was the de facto head of Rogue. While he'd thought to sacrifice her and Rogue to save his brothers, each day that went by made that outcome harder and harder to imagine. Could he betray the woman he was beginning to fall for in order to save his family? Cian was afraid he didn't know the answer anymore.

✳✳

The next night, the front door to his penthouse opened, and Danny said, "Lila's here, Mr. Mac."

Cian walked out of the kitchen, wiping his hands on a towel. "Thanks."

Danny nodded and left. Cian looked at Lila. She was dressed in her usual skinny jeans—faded and threadbare this time—paired with a black V-neck T-shirt, but she'd added a pair of dangling silver earrings, and it looked like she'd had the deep purple and blue streaks in her black hair redone. There were only a few of them, alongside one cheek, but once you'd seen them, it was as if she had a secret only you were privy to. His mind flashed to the way those stripes had looked splayed across the white pillow in his bed.

He grinned like an idiot and reached out to take her messenger bag. "Hi. Why don't I put this away?" He opened the foyer closet and set the bag inside.

"Come help?" he asked, holding a hand out toward the kitchen. She gave him a tight smile and followed.

Once in the kitchen, he pointed to some vegetables he'd been chopping. "You think you can handle those?"

She rolled her eyes. "I'm not completely incompetent in the kitchen," she retorted.

He stirred the pasta sauce he'd put together when he'd gotten home forty-five minutes earlier and put the pasta into boiling water.

"How's your mom?" he asked, looking at Lila over his shoulder. She was a quiet person, but he could tell this wasn't her normal quiet.

"She's better. Was awake a lot today and wants to go home."

"That must be a good sign, right?" He turned, leaning back against the countertop.

Lila continued chopping the carrots on the cutting board.

"Yeah. The doctors say it's going as it should."

His jaw tightened in frustration. "Lila?"

"Hmm?" She kept chopping.

"Can you put the knife down for a minute?"

She did as he asked but didn't lift her gaze.

"Are we going to talk about it?" He made his voice as gentle as he could with the need and the questions that were racing through him.

"You said it yourself," she answered. "Neither of us planned on me being here at this point. I am for now, but it doesn't really change anything."

He rubbed a hand through his hair, his heart pounding a fierce rhythm as he watched her. "I wish it changed things, though."

"How would you change things?" she asked, finally looking at him. Her eyes were filled with pain, and it was all he could do to keep from dragging her to his bed just to erase that look.

He stepped closer, laying a hand on her hip and hoping she didn't decide to make him move it. "I'd want to fall asleep beside you at night. I'd want to wake inside you in the morning." She made a small gasping sound as he skimmed his hand up the curve of her waist, then onto her arm, her shoulder, finally cupping her jaw.

"I want you," he whispered, leaning in to brush his lips against her cheek. Her breath shook as she exhaled, frozen under his touch. "I know I shouldn't.

It's selfish and dangerous, but dammit, Lila, I can't stop."

He felt the moment when she melted beneath him. Her curves arched toward him, her head tipped up, her gaze found his, and then her lips.

"It can't last," she told him as she reached for the hem of his T-shirt.

"I know." His heart raced in anticipation of her touch.

"One of us could end up dead. One of us probably *will* end up in prison."

He knew that too. Planned on it, in fact. Cian had given up on his own future long ago. He wanted Lila to have one, but as long as she insisted on staying to care for her mother, his hands were tied. As soon as she was ready, he had a beautiful beachside condo waiting for her on an island that didn't honor extradition and would be happy to have her and the ten-million-dollar bank account he'd put in her name. Assuming he wasn't forced to hand Rogue to the feds in the meantime, of course.

Then her fingertips skated across his abs, and he lost the ability to consider a future or a past or much of anything beyond the feel of her skin on his, the rasp of her breath, the heat of her most sensitive parts under his.

As he hoisted her onto the kitchen counter and devoured her mouth, he murmured things to her in Gaelic. How beautiful she was, how much he needed her, that she was the most valuable thing in his world.

"What does all that mean?" she asked, voice hoarse with need.

"That I'm falling for you Lila from Rogue." He pulled her T-shirt over her head, careful not to catch her dangling earrings.

She stopped him after he removed it, gazing at him with her dark eyes so serious.

"Don't promise me anything." She traced his lips with one finger. "Don't tell me we can be together, or that we're going to survive this. My whole life, my father broke promises to me, I'd rather not hear anything than broken promises."

He swallowed and caressed her cheek. "Okay," he whispered. "No promises. Just today. One kiss." He kissed her softly. "One touch." He cupped her breast, feeling her nipple harden beneath his palm. "One moment."

Their tongues and breath and skin tangled and strained and mixed, like a wild, totally unique dance. Denim hissed as it slid to the floor, lace and cotton whispered against the marble counters. Then he was inside her, and his world burst with a flare of light so bright, he was afraid he'd be blinded—blinded to what his brothers needed, blinded to his plans and schemes, blinded to everything but Lila. Her taste, her touch, her scent. He drove into her as she clutched him like a life raft, and the light exploded into colors, music, a universe of possibilities.

"I love you," he gasped as everything inside him tightened and she squeezed him to within an inch of his life.

"I know," she replied, desperation in each word. "I know."

Then they were both lost, and Cian made sure that even if it was only for one moment, they forgot all the bad in the world—his and hers.

**

Lila woke to the sound of men's voices in the living room. She blinked her eyes in the muted sunlight that suffused Cian's bedroom. Damn. She'd given in. Folded like a bad hand in one of her father's poker games.

She sighed, rolling to one side as she listened to the muted voices of Cian and one of his guys. With the Russians setting up shop, there was no telling what crisis they might be trying to avert now. They'd never gotten around to talking about the Russians last night, but Lila knew it was coming. The world still didn't know Xavier was gone and she was operating in his place. That meant the Russians didn't know it either, and they'd be making contact eventually. Cian was going to need her for whatever he decided to do about them. She just wasn't sure what that was going to look like yet.

She climbed out of bed, tugging down the tank top she'd slept in, and put on a pair of Cian's sweats that were draped over an armchair. They were so long and baggy, she had to roll the waistband several times to keep them up. But they were fuzzy and warm, and they made her feel almost like she was still in his embrace. After grabbing her laptop off the dresser, she hopped back on the bed and opened it up, bringing up a file of videos and clicking on the most recent one, taken nearly twenty-four hours ago.

The footage showed a man—Danny—entering Robbie MacFarlane's house, then exiting fifteen minutes later. Lila looked at the time stamp. There wasn't any rational reason Danny visiting the MacFarlane patriarch at seven thirty-two on a Tuesday morning should set off warning chimes for her, but it did. And really, since when had she ever been rational when it came to the MacFarlanes?

It had been laughably easy hacking into the security system at Robbie MacFarlane's large compound. For the most part, there was little to see. The neighborhood women coming to organize church sales with Cian's mother, the guards who were assigned to Robbie changing shifts, the three MacFarlane sons who remained in Chicago coming for weekly dinners with their parents.

And Danny. Danny visited intermittently. He was the only one of the guys who wasn't assigned to Robbie who still showed up at the house regularly. And Lila didn't know the details of Cian's business. Maybe there was some specific function Danny did that required speaking to Robbie here and there. But something about it seemed off to her, and she couldn't shake the gut instinct that it mattered.

However, while Cian had instructed her to get information on his father, he hadn't mentioned it again in several weeks now, and he definitely hadn't said, *Hack into my parents' security system*. She wasn't sure what she was seeing at Robbie's house would be information welcomed by Cian, or if he'd be so pissed she'd done it, he'd…

She stopped her train of thought. He'd what? Have her whacked?

She snorted with a burst of laughter. Cian was frightening, but he wasn't some stereotype TV mobster. And really, if she were honest with herself, Cian was anything but frightening with her. He was steely when he had to be, but there was something vulnerable about him at the same time. And she knew everything he did was for his brothers. When he'd come to her and asked for new identification and security measures for Connor, she'd seen the relief on his face. He'd wanted Connor to go, even while she knew he missed him like crazy.

She looked at the time stamp on the footage again, and then started pulling up previous footage, setting the system to search for Danny's face. Then she began recording all the times and days, looking for patterns, which was her strength. There was something here, she knew it, just as there was something in Robbie's bank accounts, and when she went to Cian, she'd have the answers. If he was pissed, then he was pissed, but he'd been the one to set her on his father, and that was because he knew something he wasn't telling her. Robbie MacFarlane was a threat to Cian or his brothers in some way, and a threat to Cian might as well be a threat to Lila, because, dammit, she loved him right back.

Chapter Five

Robbie MacFarlane brushed the USB drive aside, settling his arms on the surface of his massive wood desk. He hated goddamn technology. He could use it if he had to, but how he longed for the days when being in charge meant a gun in one hand, your enemy in the other, and a car waiting outside the back door.

"What's on it?" he asked.

"Some of Finn's greatest hits," Danny answered. "Him cleaning up the last few *events* we've had. I know how much you like to keep insurance around."

Robbie shrugged slightly in agreement. He did like to keep insurance, especially on his sons, who seemed to be less and less obedient as time went by.

"Tell me about the girl," he demanded. "The hacker."

Danny shifted in his seat, and Robbie's eyes narrowed. He could sense Danny's reluctance when it came to the woman. Yes, she was attractive, but she was just a woman. What his oldest son, and now obviously his rat, saw in her, he couldn't figure out.

"She hasn't been around that much. She's been taking care of her mom, but I think the sales on her website are going fine."

"What kind of security does Cian have on her?"

"One of us with her at all times, outside the house at night. We drive her where she needs to go, just like we do with him, Liam, and Finn."

Robbie snorted in disgust. "That kind of protection is for family only."

"Yes, sir," Danny replied. "I get the impression she's doing something more than just running the sales through Rogue."

"Yeah, she's fucking him," Robbie snarled.

Danny's look of discomfort grew. "Not very often," he muttered. "It's something other than that, something to do with the business."

"Then find out what the hell it is."

Danny nodded and stood. "Sure thing, boss," he answered lightly.

Normally, this would be when Robbie gave Danny his bonus for ratting out Cian, but Robbie wasn't feeling so generous today. It had been weeks since his youngest son, Connor, had disappeared. Nothing Danny had brought him was getting Robbie closer to finding Connor. Cian was continuing to run the family business without including Robbie, and now he didn't know what was going on between Cian and Lila.

No, Robbie wasn't feeling very generous at all.

"Get me what I want about the girl. When you do, I'll have something for you, but not until then."

Danny nodded stiffly, turned, and strode toward the door.

"And Danny?"

Danny stopped, looking warily over his shoulder at Robbie.

"Don't go getting attached to the little hacker," Robbie warned. "She may not be around forever."

**

Katya sat on a mattress on the floor, her ribs throbbing as the waning light filtered in from the high windows in the room she and Nadja now shared with only five other girls. Her second beating had been brutal, and days later, she was still discovering new places that hurt.

"You can't do that again," Nadja scolded from behind her as she braided Katya's damp hair, being extra gentle, her voice thick with emotion.

"I may not be able to stop them, but I won't make it easy for them—or enjoyable," Katya snapped.

Nadja stopped her ministrations and leaned around Katya's shoulder so she could look her in the face. Katya couldn't help but notice the dark circles that had appeared under her friend's eyes along with the slight tremble in her hands.

"I thought you were dead this time," Nadja whispered. "Please don't do it again."

Katya smiled at the only thing in her life that mattered now. "You don't need to worry about me. I know how far I can push. I'm worth too much. It's the boobs," she announced, plumping both with her hands.

Nadja shook her head but smirked at the same time before she went back to braiding Katya's hair. Katya secretly breathed a sigh of relief. Upsetting

Nadja was the last thing she wanted to do. It was obvious they were feeding Nadja drugs, and if Katya was right, her friend was already addicted.

It made the need to escape even more essential. Unbidden, the image of a big, broad man flickered through her head. Blue eyes, a tattoo peeking out the collar of his T-shirt. The smell of his warm leather jacket when he'd held it out to her.

She closed her eyes and tried not to regret her decision. She could have been out—away—and the thought had occurred to her afterward that if she'd done it, she could have gone to the police, told them about the other girls, maybe gotten some help to rescue Nadja. But in Katya's world, the world of post-Communist Russia, police were owned by the same men who held her captive. What was to say the police in Chicago, USA were any different?

And what if the man who'd offered to rescue her had only wanted to take her to another place just like this one? No, it had been too big a risk to take. She couldn't leave Nadja on so little possibility. She had to get them both out, or it wouldn't be worth escaping at all.

She closed her eyes and tried not to think about the pain in her ribs, focusing on the feeling of Nadja's fingers in her hair. And later on, when Nadja had been allowed to shower as well, she returned the favor and braided Nadja's hair, then she put her arms around her friend's thin shoulders and held her as Nadja shook with the need for the next fix.

That was when Katya decided—she was going to find a way out. Or she was going to die trying.

Chapter Six

"Shit," Liam whispered to himself as he watched two well-armed Russian guards position themselves on either side of the entrance to the brothel.

He'd been busy all day with organizing distribution, a job that used to belong to Connor. Since Connor left, he and Finn had been sharing the responsibilities. Finn had set up a new and better way to do it, but it still required they check up. The guys who took the product to the streets were often only one step above junkies themselves, and they needed a lot of monitoring to ensure they didn't take shortcuts that could put everyone in jail.

As a result of the babysitting, he was later getting to the brick building on East Twenty-Third than he'd intended. He'd missed the window between seven and ten p.m., and now there were Bratva men everywhere.

He crouched in the darkened portal of the shuttered slaughterhouse across the street and debated his options. He could come back another night. It was the logical thing to do. The smart thing. The safe thing.

But for days now, all he'd seen when he went to bed at night were the haunted eyes of Katya—Katerina—as she sat defiantly in that chair and insisted she wouldn't leave without her friend.

She was courageous in a way he'd not found many women to be. Oh yeah, he knew it was sexist, and it wasn't that he didn't think women could be—after all, Connor's girlfriend, Jess, had endured a solid beating from Vasquez soldiers before she and Connor had gotten away from the family business and Chicago. But Liam didn't meet many women in his line of work, and the ones he did were party girls at clubs or the women who belonged to his men.

His relations with women were either polite distance—wives and mothers in the neighborhood—or quick fucking—drunk girls in storage closets or bar bathrooms. He had to admit, he hadn't given many women the opportunity to be real and courageous.

But Katya, there she'd been, having recently been beaten, undoubtedly raped too, and she had a chance to get out, but she'd turned it down.

Of course, from her perspective, the men who were known might have been preferable to the unknown—him.

He scrubbed a hand over his scalp as he watched two more men approach the door to the warehouse. They said a few words to the guards, then were admitted.

Dammit. It wasn't like him to be indecisive. Either he was going to do this or he wasn't, but hiding across the street wasn't going to make it any easier.

He took a deep breath and closed his eyes. That haunted face reappeared before him, and the decision was no longer his to make.

"Shit," he muttered again, before quietly moving out of the doorway and walking away from the warehouse, down the block, and around the corner toward the only gas station in the area. His car was parked there. He was going to need it.

**

Nadya had been the first one taken from their room that night, and Katya was, as usual, sick with worry. What if they gave her too much of the drugs? What if Nadya was so out of it, she couldn't defend herself? What if they overdosed her? Their captors had a few basic standards—no marks on the face—but they allowed men to give the girls all sorts of drugs, and Nadja was in no position to decide how much she could take of anything.

And only two nights ago, a girl had been smothered to death by the man who'd bought her. Katya had heard the man screaming for mercy when Sergei, the big boss, beat him until he agreed to pay the full value of the girl—twenty thousand US dollars.

The rooms they kept for the women to *entertain* in were sparse—a bed, a nightstand, a mirror, and a few basic toys—a strap-on dildo, a blindfold, some edible lotions. And of course, plenty of lube and condoms. The Bratva were very specific that they had no use for pregnant women nor diseased ones. But all a man needed to *kill* a woman were his two bare hands.

The door opened, and Katya and the other three girls who were in the room all turned stiff with terror. "You three," the man named Petrov ordered, pointing to Katya and two other blondes. "Come with me."

Katya swallowed the bile and stood, lifting her chin and ignoring the appraising look Alexei gave her as she walked past him in the doorway.

"You'd better behave yourself tonight, *suka*, or you might not make it to see tomorrow." He smacked her on the ass, and she hissed at him like a snake.

Alexei laughed as they moved down the hall. When they reached the end, another guard outside one of the rooms they entertained in told them to walk inside, turn around once slowly, then come back out.

The room was bigger and fancier than the ones Katya had seen before. It had a carpet on the floor, an attached bathroom, and furniture beyond just the large bed.

Katya was the last in line and didn't see the man sitting in the low-slung modern armchair until she was right in front of him. He sat loosely, a glass of something amber dangling from his fingertips. His knees were spread wide, jeans and heavy boots covering his lower half, while a plain white T-shirt fit snug against his massive chest. He sat like a king on a throne, and while his eyes were covered with a pair of reflective sunglasses and his buzz-cut hair was obscured by a Chicago Cubs cap, she'd know him anywhere.

She glared at him, feeling betrayed he'd come back to take advantage after his offer to rescue her. She'd been right to refuse his so-called help. He was no better than the rest of them. Any remaining fantasies she'd had about America dissolved right then and there. There were no good men anywhere, not in Russia, not in Chicago, USA. Men only wanted one thing, and they didn't care if you were willing to give it or not.

She couldn't tell if he was watching her face, but she mouthed a Russian profanity at him and pivoted to walk away as quickly as possible.

"That one," he said behind her, his voice deep and gritty.

Alexei watched the other girls walk out ahead of her but blocked her exit.

"He picked you," he said, flashing her a grin. "You'll redeem yourself this way. He's paying triple the usual executive rate. Make sure you earn it." He leaned close, his breath fetid as he got right in her face. "You fuck this up and your next stop is the dumpster out back." Then he laughed, and slammed the door in her face.

**

Liam sat watching the young woman as she stood, head bowed, facing the door, refusing to turn and look at him.

He hoisted himself out of the chair and walked partway to where she stood.

She was in lingerie again, tiny pink satin shorts and a matching camisole, and while he didn't want to be an asshole, he couldn't help but notice her long legs and pert ass. She was thin and graceful, like a ballerina, her wavy hair in a loose braid down her back.

"Do you want the rest of this drink? It's safe. I had some. But we don't have a lot of time, so you need to drink up quick."

She spun around, her eyes practically shooting flames.

"We don't have a lot of time?" she snapped in her exotic accent. "Don't you have money for full hour? Or maybe you think I'm not worth hour? You are only thinking it's fun to try the one who bit a man's cock?"

Liam tried not to grin at her fury. She wasn't short, but she looked as though she'd blow over with a strong wind. Yet she had all the conviction and passion he'd been privy to when he'd first found her, and it made him secretly pleased they hadn't broken her yet. Because she was sort of amazing.

"I'd guess you're worth a hell of a lot more than the hour I just paid for, and while the idea of having my dick bitten is oddly intriguing, I'm actually just here to get you out."

She blinked at him, her blue feline eyes framed by dark lashes that looked as though someone had smudged charcoal on them.

"Get me out?"

"Yes," he said, holding the glass of bourbon out to her. She shook her head stubbornly, and he shrugged, swallowing the rest of it in one shot.

He set the glass down on the end table next to the chair he'd been sitting in. "I should have taken you with me when I was here the other day. I realized it thirty minutes after I left."

"I told you I cannot go without my friend."

He pursed his lips. "Yeah, I understand, I really do, but I can't manage that yet." She started to open that wide, full mouth but he stopped her, shaking his head emphatically. "No, not today. But I give you my word, I'll work to get her out as soon as possible. My brothers and I have a lot of resources at our disposal. We'll get her, but not tonight."

Katya scowled, arms crossed under her ample breasts. "I don't even know who you are," she argued.

Liam knew time was of the essence, and he didn't have enough to placate this woman. She was fierce, and that was admirable but also a pain in the ass.

He walked past her and opened the door, leaning out to look at the hall. One of the guards was a few feet to the right, sitting in a chair playing a game on his phone. He stood and began lumbering toward Liam. "You need something?"

Liam smiled benignly until the man got close enough, then he swung hard and fast, knocking the guy back a few feet as his fist connected with jawbone. He followed it up with a booted kick to the man's nuts, then brought both fists down on the back of the guard's head, sending him sprawling to the floor, out cold.

He could hear Katya's gasp as he squatted and took the guard's gun out of his shoulder holster. He stood and looked at her where she was gaping in the doorway to their room.

"Two choices," he said. "Come quietly, or I'll carry you out ass first. The second way's more likely to get us both killed."

She swallowed, her eyes large as she looked at the guard on the floor, then back at him. Finally, he held out his hand, and she tentatively took it.

"Good choice," he murmured, then pulled her

down the hall toward the staircase that led to the upstairs window he knew was still ajar.

Chapter Seven

"Now what?" Robbie MacFarlane snarled as Danny came sauntering up to him where he sat holding court at the pub he'd owned for three decades.

"Need to talk to you," Danny said, his face communicating nothing. "Cian sent me."

Robbie nodded to the other men at the table, all old colleagues who'd worked for the Dublin Devils in one capacity or another over the years. He'd always run staffing loose, allowing men to leave his employ if they had a good reason. In his experience, it was just as valuable to have friends who owed you outside the organization as it was to have men who worked for you inside it.

After he'd cleared the table, he motioned to Danny to take a seat.

"Liam called a meeting with Cian and Finn at about midnight last night," Danny began without preamble. "They all came to Cian's place. I was on overnight shift."

Robbie grunted. His oldest son lived in a trendy penthouse in another part of town. Robbie wondered how often Cian remembered that it was he—the man Cian disdained so heartily—who had paid for that fancy condo.

"He brought along a friend," Danny said, a smirk fully in place.

"Well, get on with it, then."

"A girl. Blonde, hot, and Russian."

Robbie blinked at his spy. "What?"

"Apparently, there's a new Russian whorehouse in town. Liam went to try it out and came back with a door prize." He chuckled.

Robbie didn't find anything about the situation to be funny.

"There's goddamn Russians in town?" he asked, incredulous.

"Yep. And they're trafficking women from overseas." He looked longingly at Robbie's tumbler of whiskey.

Robbie gritted his teeth and motioned for the girl he had waiting tables to get Danny a drink.

"So what the hell was he doing with the girl? He pay for her or steal her?"

Danny took the drink he was served and downed half of it in one gulp. "Don't know for sure. But Cian was pissed as hell at him, and Liam and the girl stayed at Cian's place the rest of the night. Finn went home after about an hour."

Robbie snorted. His third son, Finn, was supposedly the brains of the bunch. But he was also soft. Quiet, always thinking. He didn't even carry a gun most of the time. What kind of a man in their line of work didn't carry a gun?

"You need to find out everything," Robbie instructed. "If Liam's gotten sideways with the Russians, I want to know about it."

"Sure thing."

"What about Cian and the girl from Rogue?" He watched Danny for any sign of the previous squeamishness at the mention of the hacker, but Danny was a good soldier. He'd gotten the message last time they'd talked. He coughed up the information with no hesitation.

"They had a sleepover a couple of nights ago. He hasn't seen her since."

Robbie's lips twisted up in a wry smile. "Good. As long as he's fucking her, she's leverage." He stood and donned the black jacket. "Find out what's going on with the Russians. I don't want them in my town, and Cian's not up to the job of getting them out."

Danny gave a quick nod as he polished off his whiskey.

As Robbie turned to walk away, Danny stopped him. "Hey, boss?"

Robbie looked at the big bodyguard over his shoulder.

"You find him yet?" Danny asked, head tilted to the side like a slightly curious dog.

Robbie's whole soul darkened with anger. When Robbie got his hands on Connor, not even his beautiful wife, Angela, would be able to protect the kid.

"No," he answered brusquely. "But I got the rest of my life to keep looking."

**

As she opened her eyes, Katya had a moment of panic. Her heart raced, and she gasped, sitting up and looking around frantically, searching for something she could use to protect herself.

Then everything came into focus, and her pulse relaxed, her breathing returning to normal. The bedroom was sparse—some weights in one corner, a dresser, leather armchair, the king-size bed she was in—all the furniture in black, plain white sheer curtains on the large glass door that opened to a small balcony.

As she got her bearings, she could hear him in the other room talking on the phone. Liam MacFarlane, the man who'd taken her out of the whorehouse.

"She's still sleeping, but I'll bring her by in a bit….yeah, yesterday I just let her watch TV and eat whatever she wanted. She's still pretty scared, but hopefully today, she'll tell us a few things."

He paused, then his voice dropped, and she couldn't hear the rest of the conversation. She swung her legs over the edge of the large bed and stood, looking at the stack of clothes he'd taken her to buy the day before. He'd been a perfect gentleman so far, making sure she had everything she needed, giving her the bed and sleeping on the big sofa in his living room, not pressuring her for anything, just letting her be. But she still didn't trust him. He was a mobster, like the men who'd stolen her. Why would he be nice unless he expected something eventually? Something she undoubtedly wouldn't want to give.

She slipped on a pair of black track pants with the black tank top she'd worn to bed, then covered up with a hoodie before taking a deep breath and opening the door.

"Hey," Liam said from his perch at the kitchen counter where he was drinking a cup of coffee and reading a newspaper. It was an incongruous sight—the burly guy in a white sleeveless T-shirt and gray sweats, a *Chicago Sun-Times* in one hand and a cup that read *Luck o' the Irish* in the other.

"You hungry?" he asked.

She crossed her arms in front of her protectively. She'd noticed the day before that he never got too close to her, and when he stayed on the stool instead of approaching her, she nodded slightly.

"Yes. Please."

He smiled casually and made his way into the kitchen. When there was a counter between them, she moved and took a seat next to the one he'd been occupying at the bar top.

"Did you sleep all right?" He cracked some eggs in a bowl before whisking them.

"Yes."

His gaze darted to her. "I told you yesterday I'd answer any questions you have about what's going on. Do you have any?"

She swallowed, carefully watching his movements around the kitchen. She was starving; she needed to eat. She'd refused dinner the night before because they were eating here at his home. She'd eaten lunch only because it had been a hot dog at a Target store where she knew he couldn't slip something into it.

Once he'd poured the egg mixture into the pan, he handed her a glass of orange juice, then leaned back against the refrigerator watching her.

She drank the entire glass of juice, the acid

burning her esophagus as it moved down.

Setting the glass on the counter, she finally complied with his request. "Why?" she asked. "Why did you take me? And what are you going to do with me?"

He stirred the scrambled eggs before turning down the heat on the gas burner.

"I took you because I couldn't stop thinking about you in that place." He had the decency to look repulsed when he mentioned the brothel. "And because you have information that could be helpful to us. The Russians are trying to take over my family's territory and we need all the information we can get to keep them out." He paused, looking away from her. "We don't condone slavery. We won't allow it in our city."

She didn't say anything else while he scraped her eggs onto a plate and handed them to her. She was still wary of eating or drinking anything he'd prepared, but she also knew she'd never be able to escape if she was weak with hunger.

Taking the plate, she set it down and took one small bite, chewing while he watched her. She swallowed, then asked, "But I am prisoner here with you too? I cannot walk out the door?"

"Where would you go? You have no immigration papers, no money, and if the Russians saw you, they'd kill you on the spot. I'm not keeping you a prisoner, I'm protecting you."

She snorted softly before giving in and shoveling the eggs in her mouth as fast as she could.

"So I give you information, then what? You say it—I have no papers, no money, nothing. You will kill me then?"

He shook his head. "Of course not. I don't kill women or civilians—you're both."

"And what of Nadja?" she finally asked. She'd spent the previous day so shell-shocked, she hadn't been able to focus on anything but surviving. As Liam had politely helped her get some essentials and allowed her to rest, she'd been terrified each and every moment. Not knowing what he was going to do next, not trusting a word he said. But this morning, after a night's sleep, she knew she couldn't forget Nadja. Nadja would think she was dead. She would be inconsolable.

For the first time since he'd broken down the door where she was imprisoned after the beating, she sensed doubt in him. His gaze fell to the floor for a moment as he leaned back, his arm muscles bunching in the sleeveless shirt. When he looked at her again, his gaze was dark, and her heart beat fast, but not in the same way it did when Alexei or Sergei looked at her that way.

"I'm not sure." Her heart sank. But as much as she wanted to damn him for taking her away from Nadja, she was here, sitting in sunlight, having slept in a real bed and showered without fearing one of Sergei's guards would try to get a freebie. She couldn't bring herself to hate him.

"I don't have a plan for how to get her out, Katya," he admitted, his expression full of sympathy. "We're going to be at war with the Russians now, and it would require a major military-grade operation to get back in that building and take her."

She swallowed. She'd sworn from the first time they'd shoved her into a room with a strange man that she wouldn't cry. She'd never give them the satisfaction of seeing her break, and she wouldn't give it to this man either, but the idea of never seeing Nadja again made her want to. It made her feel as though she'd been given a glimpse of the sun, then someone had drawn the curtains, leaving her in cold, black desolation.

"And what about me?" she asked in a small voice.

"You'll have to go somewhere away from here, but not back to Russia. They'll be looking for you, and they won't stop."

Something inside her did break then, something that even the men who'd raped her hadn't been able to destroy. Katya had been many things in her short life—poor, hungry, desperate, afraid. But she'd never been alone, and now she realized she was. Because whether Russia was perfect or not, it was her home. Whether Paula was perfect or not, she was her mother. And whether Nadja was weak or not, she was her best friend.

Now she had none of them, and she was probably not going to ever get them back. But she wouldn't cry. No, she wouldn't cry.

Instead, she did what she'd done every day since Sergei had shoved her into that van. She ground her teeth, breathed deep, and gave Liam MacFarlane her haughtiest gaze.

"If it is last thing I ever do," she spat, "I will make them pay for all of it. I will make them pay for taking everything from me."

**

Liam looked at the beautiful young woman glaring at

him as if she could burn him alive with her eyes alone. She'd told him she was twenty-four, the same age as his youngest brother, Connor, and eight years younger than him. He knew he'd slept with women her age, but she was different somehow. Less worldly, yet also more worn. Vulnerable in a way he wasn't used to, yet with a spark and a steel that almost made him…proud.

"I'll do it for you," he promised. "You don't need that on your conscience. Know that I'll do whatever it takes to make them pay for what they did to you, and to Nadja. And I won't let them find you," he added softly, trying to reassure her. "We'll have to figure out where to send you, give you a new identity. We can do that."

She relaxed a touch, and not for the first time in the last few days, he wondered exactly what they had done to her. It was a foregone conclusion she'd been raped, and he knew she'd been beaten, but the devil was in the details. How many times? How violently? Conscious? Unconscious? Was she tortured? Drugged?

Liam had been the chief enforcer in his family for nearly ten years. He knew about torture, both the giving and the receiving. He knew about being imprisoned, as well as about taking prisoners. And he knew that Katya wasn't that different from a cornered animal right now. She was terrified, bruised, battered, and didn't trust anyone. He could see it in her eyes. It was why he'd kept his distance, making sure to give her ample space, never moving too fast or doing anything she might perceive as threatening.

"But now you need information?" She looked longingly at her empty plate.

He quietly reached across the counter and took the plate away, replacing it with a bottled smoothie he took out of the fridge. "Open it," he instructed when she simply stared at it. "You need the calories."

She cracked the seal on the cap, and he saw relief wash over her as she took several healthy swallows of the chocolate-flavored smoothie.

"Yes, we need information. Anything and everything you saw or heard while they had you. It might not seem important to you but could give us a clue that helps us run them out of town."

She finished the smoothie and belched. Her eyes widened in shock at the sound, and her cheeks turned pink almost instantly.

Liam laughed as she continued from pink to crimson.

"*Idi k chertu*," she snapped, glaring.

"Sweetheart, I don't know what you just said, but you don't need to be embarrassed in front of me. I grew up with three brothers. There's no sound or smell you could make that would surprise me."

She tried to keep a straight face, giving him her fiercest look, but then she cracked, a throaty laugh breaking free as a grin spread across her face. Liam felt the sound reverberate through him like some sort of slow wave rolling into shore. His own grin grew, and she laughed harder, collapsing onto the counter in front of her, gasping for breath as her eyes began to water.

Liam watched her, fascinated by the first unguarded emotion she'd shown since he'd taken her out of that hellhole. Her golden hair was a disheveled mess, she didn't wear a speck of makeup, and she was possibly the most beautiful thing he'd ever laid eyes on.

When her laughter finally subsided, she wiped the tears from her eyes, little aftershocks of giggles coming every few seconds as she tried to regain control.

"I'm sorry," she said. Then she sobered, her mind taking her somewhere else for a moment. "I don't think I laugh since I came to America," she added softly.

"I'm glad I could be of service." He kept smiling. He never smiled this much, but damn. That laugh.

He turned and retrieved a pot of coffee he'd brewed before she woke. "It's still warm," he offered, showing it to her.

She hesitated for only a second before nodding. He poured her a cup.

"Cream or sugar?"

She snorted. "I'm Russian. We drink the coffee that is…" She struggled for the English word. "Powdered?"

"Instant?" Liam asked, disgust causing him to wrinkle his nose.

"Yes. That. Instant. If you put milk, it taste like milk. I don't like milk."

"That's because instant coffee is hardly better than toilet water," Liam scolded. "Drink some of that. That's what coffee is supposed to taste like."

She took a sip, her eyes growing wide. He waited for her to gag or demand the cream, but instead, she smiled, taking a larger swallow.

"*Da*. This is much better. I like this."

Katya liked coffee. And God help him, Liam liked her.

Chapter Eight

"So basically Liam risked his neck to pull her out, and all she could tell us was a few first names and the way they have the place set up."

Lila watched as Cian paced in front of the window of his condo. His slacks were black, his knit shirt a shade of blue that she'd describe as azure. It matched his eyes, and try as hard as she might, she didn't think she'd ever forget the exact shade of his eyes as long as she lived.

"He did a good thing, though," she added as Cian stopped and turned to face her. "I know you're upset he took such a big risk, but you saw Katya. Can you imagine what it must have been like for her in there?"

Cian sighed before walking over and sitting on the sofa next to her. Not too close, but not far enough either. Lila had no idea where the two of them stood after their most recent night together, but she knew the closer Cian got, the more it scared her.

"I can't think about it," Cian said softly. "I'm trying to balance so much here. I can't think about what those girls are going through. It's…" He swallowed, his gaze leaving hers for just a moment. "Beyond horrible. And I can't help them, so I can't think about it."

Her chest contracted the smallest bit, and she broke her own rule that she'd made just that morning at breakfast by reaching out and putting her fingertips on his arm. "I know. You can't save everyone. You have to put your family first."

He stared at her for a long breath, something in his eyes so disquieted, she wondered what she'd said wrong.

He finally released a shaky breath. "Yeah. The family has to come first," he murmured before he shifted, reaching out to run a finger down her cheek. "Will you keep helping me with the Russians, Lila from Rogue?"

She couldn't smother the ghost of a smile that spread over her lips at his nickname for her. The first time she'd ever texted with him, she'd introduced herself that way. He'd never let her live it down.

"I'll feed them whatever information you want under the guise of being Xavier. But that's not what you mean, is it?"

He sat up straighter, pulling away, and she knew it was back to business. Because Cian never left business behind for long.

"Finn has come up with a plan," he began, leaning back and putting one booted foot over the opposite knee. "We have to get the Russians out of town. But conventional warfare won't work with them. We need to hit them in a way they won't expect from us—beat them at their own game. Finn wants to wage cyberwar."

Lila blinked. Before she'd gotten the relatively stable job setting up systems for Rogue, she'd done a lot of hacking for a lot of people, but she'd never been involved in a war of the type Cian was describing.

"Oh-kay," she said slowly. "Do you understand what that entails?"

He flashed a smile. "That's what you're going to tell me, right?"

Sighing, Lila crossed her legs under her on the sofa. She knew Cian would grasp the overall effort, he was a bright guy, an exceptional businessman. But he didn't know tech, and she wasn't sure there was any way to fully explain to him the vulnerabilities you risked if you went to war.

"It means I'll be hacking into their systems—repeatedly. I'll access anything I can, destroy anything I find, steal cash from banks, lock them out of their own accounts, discover personal information, and give that to you to use as you see fit."

"And?" he prompted when she paused.

"And it will put Rogue at risk, put me at risk, and put your family at risk."

She settled a little farther into the plush leather cushions.

"The more active I am, the bigger the odds I'll be tracked by the feds as well as the Russians. When you focus a lot of attention on a group of systems with a common link, like say this Sergei who's heading up the Russians, it makes it more likely you'll get caught. It shows a pattern, provides a trail for the feds and others to follow."

"Let's say, for the sake of argument, the feds knew what you were doing ahead of time and agreed not to go after you. Would you feel better about it, then?"

Lila snorted. "Considering the feds don't know I exist, I'd have to say no."

"They know you exist, Lila. You've got to be on their most wanted list. You're one of the best in the world."

"I'm also completely anonymous. The handle I used to hack under has been dead and buried for years, and no one's ever investigated me as my real self. The feds have never been able to get anything on Rogue, but if they were alerted to me messing with the Russians, they'd start watching me, and eventually, they're bound to follow that to Rogue."

Cian's jaw flexed in what looked like frustration.

"Look, I can't just allow the Russians to come into town and do what they please. I haven't even told my father they're here, but he'll find out sooner than later, and then what? It's either go to their whorehouse with semiautos and blow the place to hell, or go after them another way. The guns will only ensure they send more soldiers from New York, and I don't have an army big enough for that."

He leaned toward her, his voice dropping. "I've told my *friends* the Russians are in town. I'll give them anything I can to help them take the Russians out."

He glanced around as if, even in his living room, someone might hear him. Luckily for him, Lila had secured his laptop and his Wi-Fi networks, and had the place swept every forty-eight hours since she'd discovered Xavier was spying on Cian.

"But," he continued, "you know my friends don't

work fast. All their damn rules mean they might not be able to do anything to stop the Bratva from gaining a stronghold. And I can't be seen as though I'm not taking action. I have to make war this time, Lila. And I can't do it without you."

And there it was. Lila's heart hurt with it. With the patterns her life persisted in following. She thought when she finally did her last bad deed for her father, she'd unloaded that particular baggage, but lately, she'd come to realize she'd only traded him in for other bad men who asked her to do bad things. Other hackers, clients at Rogue, Xavier. And now, Cian.

Except everything in Lila said Cian wasn't like the rest. He was different—a criminal, yes, but a complicated one—a strange combination of considerate and cold, conscientious and cryptic. Some days, she was convinced she needed to get away from him forever. Others, she thought she might never recover from him.

"Okay," she answered simply, when it was anything but. "But I need help with Rogue. And I'll need some expensive hardware. It's going to cost you."

"You know money's never an issue. Anything you want."

She sighed, moving to stand from the sofa.

"Hey." He put a hand on her arm, his fingertips warming her wrist like tiny sparks of hope. "Can you stay for dinner? I'll order something in."

She raised an eyebrow. "And after dinner?"

He leaned over, running his lips across the arch of her jaw before inhaling her hair. Shivers ran up and down her spine as other parts of her tingled and warmed.

"After dinner, I'm going to ask you to have a sleepover." He kissed her tenderly on the corner of her mouth.

"What are we doing here, Cian?" She asked softly, her head bowed.

He pulled back and looked her in the eyes, his face serious and so beautiful. "We're trying to remember we're alive," he answered before he pulled her to him and pressed his mouth to hers.

**

"Play it again," Sergei demanded as he leaned over the younger man's laptop. On screen, the big man, dressed like any gangbanger off the street with a dark baseball cap, white T-shirt, and dark wash jeans, pulled the woman down the hallway, turning at the stairwell. The man had known those stairs were there and had gone out a window on the second floor. He'd been in the building before. At last, Sergei had the answer to who had broken down the door to the room where he'd been keeping his most rebellious girl.

There was always that one woman. The one who simply wouldn't comply and accept her new reality. Sergei looked forward to those women, actually. They provided him with hours of entertainment. But this one had ended up being more than just a handful of trouble.

"*Sukin syn*," Sergei snarled before slamming a hand down on the desk. He'd watched the tape of the man over and over, and he couldn't see enough of the man's face to know who it had been. He'd combed through the footage thoroughly, but still nothing. And his fucking worthless employees had nothing either. It was most likely someone sent by the MacFarlanes, but he couldn't afford to assume anything. He needed evidence.

"Sir," one of his useless employees said as he leaned his head in the door. "Alexei is here, and he thinks he might have found something new."

"Well, don't just stand there!" Sergei shouted. "Get him in here."

Alexei took the other man's place in a flash, stepping into the suite and closing the door behind himself.

"What did you find?" Sergei asked immediately.

"We talk to contacts in the city. We took this photo"—he held up a still shot from the video Sergei had been watching —"and showed it around. No one wanted to say a name, but with a little persuasion"— he grinned—"we were able to get one. Liam MacFarlane."

Sergei felt a burning rage simmer in his belly. "The enforcer, yes?"

"*Da.*" Alexei nodded. "They are afraid of him. He is known to be…formidable."

Turning to the man at the computer, Sergei leaned down, looking at the video where it was frozen on screen. "I want everything on Liam MacFarlane. Where he lives, where he drinks, where he takes a shit and when. I will hunt him until he is left with nowhere to hide, and then I will make him pay for this. The MacFarlanes will submit, and Liam will be how I make them do it."

**

Cian sat in the dark of his office at Banshee, watching the glow of the computer screen in front of him. It had been three days since Liam had taken the woman out of the whorehouse, and still no response from the Russians.

But he knew it was coming, and he knew they'd hit Liam first. He needed to find a way to make his obstinate brother go to a safe house before the Russians found him. Liam was sitting around at his apartment with a couple of guys outside the door, like a sitting duck. And the fact there was a pretty blonde there distracting him didn't help.

He leaned his head back against his chair. For sixteen years, he'd watched Liam mold himself into the man he was today. And Cian wasn't dumb. He knew how it had happened and why. After Cian's eighteenth birthday, the night he and Liam had discovered who their father truly was, Liam had begun a campaign to be the brute their old man seemed to want. He'd done everything he could to bulk up, dumb down, and adopt the outlook on life Robbie MacFarlane had so wanted *Cian* to have.

At first, Cian had thought Liam was doing it to win Robbie's approval, but it didn't take long to realize Liam was doing it to buffer Cian. His younger brother, still just a kid when Robbie's cruelty became unbearable, had taken on the role of family enforcer not to please Robbie or because he loved violence, but to protect Cian. To ensure Cian never again had to face a choice like he'd made that night when their father had pointed the gun at Liam's head.

Cian's chest tightened at the memory. He hadn't folded when Robbie had threatened *him*, but when

Robbie threatened *Liam*, he'd made the only choice he could—someone else's life instead of his brother's. And in return, Liam had given up everything to stand by Cian's side, to have Cian's back, and to guard Cian's front.

As if conjured by his thoughts, his phone chimed with a message about Liam.

This is Ricky. There's been an explosion at Liam's place. Whole building is being evacuated. I was doing the coffee run. Can't get back in.

Cian's heart nearly beat out of its cage as he stood and began moving.

"Danny! Louis!" he shouted as he ran for the door. He sprinted down the hallway, breathless not from exertion but from panic. His lungs felt as though they were encased in concrete, each breath an excruciating effort.

He reached the bar where his guards were playing a game of war while they drank a pitcher of beer.

"Bomb," Cian gasped as he hit the room running. "At Liam's."

Danny and Louis both tossed their cards on the table and were up, grabbing jackets off chair backs so fast, they knocked the chairs over, the table rocking in the melee.

"We got you." Danny pushed past Cian, heading toward the back parking lot. "Don't move until I've swept the car. It won't do any good for *you* to get blown to bits trying to see if *he's* been blown to bits."

Louis put a hand on Cian's back as Cian bent over, palms on the table that held the remains of their card game. He gasped for breath, furious he couldn't get control of it. He looked weak in front of his men, and there was no room for that—ever.

"It's okay," Louis said quietly. "He's tough, and he's the best at this stuff. He'll come walking out of there wondering why anyone was worried."

Cian nodded, concentrating on his breathing, trying to will his racing heart to relax.

"Finn," he gasped.

"On it." Louis pulled a phone from his pocket and shot off a text.

A moment later, Louis's phone chimed, and he read it off to Cian. "He's on his way to Liam's. His guys will sweep the car first."

Cian nodded, finally able to stand. His right hand shook, so he shoved it in his front pants pocket.

Danny came back in, walking quickly, a phone in hand. "It's all good. We can go."

Cian strode out of the bar and down the hall, regaining some of his typical confidence and implacable demeanor. Damn, he hated to have someone see him as weak. But if Liam was dead, he'd be a much weaker man forever.

**

He was falling, everything black except for the dust that clawed at his throat, clouded his lungs, and coated his skin. In the back of his mind, he knew there was something he needed to be doing, but everything was dusty, and there was a humming in his ears that wouldn't go away.

But one sound began to distinguish itself from the white noise inside his head. It was a small whimper, like a kitten or a baby. It turned to moans, then one word: "Help."

Liam's eyes rolled open, and he coughed, blinking at the strange light that filtered through the space. His lungs were on fire, but when he tried to sit up, his ribs answered with a shock of pain that made sparks dance in front of his eyes.

"Fuck," he groaned as he cautiously rolled to one side, then pushed himself up to sitting, one arm banded across his torso to hold his ribs steady.

That was when he heard it again. The quiet plea for help. Katya. His mind finally cleared, and he looked around at what had been the apartment below his. The blast had been small, but big enough to collapse the floor and send both of them plummeting ten feet down.

He gingerly moved his legs, pleased to find they didn't seem to be injured, then stood, still gasping at the pain in his ribs.

"Katya?" His voice was raspy with the dust that floated through the air. "Katya, I'm here. Where are you?"

He heard a murmur and turned in a three-hundred-sixty-degree rotation, eyes scanning the chunks of concrete, overturned furniture and broken glass everywhere. God help them if anyone had been in the apartment when the ceiling collapsed.

Then he saw a flash of blonde behind an armoire of some sort turned on its side near the wall. He moved his poor bruised body as fast as he could and peered over the armoire, which came up to his chin. There she was, sprawled against the wall, one ankle disturbingly swollen, her blonde hair coated in gray dust, her face scrunched in pain.

"Hey," he said, and she opened her eyes.

"Tell me what hurts." He looked at the armoire

and tried to figure out how he'd move it to get her out of the little prison.

"It's the foot—" She paused as she shifted and grimaced. "The part above the foot."

"Your ankle?" he asked.

"Yes." She released a breath that sounded like relief. "My ankle."

"Anything else?"

"No. Nothing that matters."

"Okay," he coached. "I think I've broken a couple of ribs, so I can't move this thing, but if you can stand, maybe we can bring you over the top of it?"

She eyed him doubtfully.

"We have to try. The police and firefighters will be coming through here in no time, and I don't want to get taken in for questioning. It's not going to end well for me once they realize who I am."

She blinked at him once with her pretty blue eyes, then nodded in understanding.

"Okay. I do it." She put her good leg underneath her with her back against the wall and pushed up. She grunted with the effort, but managed to stand using only the one leg, then she leaned forward, placing her hands on the armoire for balance, her injured leg holding no weight.

"Are there any knobs or shelves in this thing you can use to help climb on top?" Liam asked. "Once you're up, I can get you down this other side."

"Yes." Katya looked at her side of the armoire. "Very small knobs on the drawers."

"Okay. Put your hands up here as far as you can."

She did as he asked, and he grabbed her hands

across the wood surface, holding her wrists as tightly as he could, gritting his teeth as pain attacked his midsection.

"Now, I won't let you fall, so lean on this thing and lift your good foot onto the drawer knobs."

He felt when both her feet had left the floor. She pulled on his arms, and he braced himself, trying to let the armoire hold as much of the weight as possible so his poor ribs wouldn't burst into flames.

Then the weight lightened.

"Okay," she gasped, balancing with her armpits now up to the edge of the armoire.

He looked at her, eyes on a level now. "Hi," he said, giving her a small smile. "Fancy seeing you here."

She stared at him blankly. "You are strange man," she answered, and he chuckled softly.

"Probably."

"Now what do I do?"

"Is there another drawer knob higher up?"

"No."

Dammit. He took a breath and let it out slowly, hearing sirens and commotion outside the building. They were running out of time.

"You're going to have to let me drag you the rest of the way. Just push off the knob as much as you can, and I'll pull."

She looked less than convinced. "You are hurt. That will be very painful."

"I'll live." He looked at where the armoire was pressing against her chest. "It's probably not going to feel so great to you either." His gaze dropped to her breasts, crushed against the wood. "You're going to take the brunt of this right on your chest."

"I have felt worse," she replied sharply, and Liam shuddered.

"On three. One. Two. Three." He pulled as hard as he could, and she skidded up and over the top of the armoire until she was lying on her stomach, balanced on the damn thing.

"*Der'mo!*" she spat in pain while she splayed across the hard wood.

Liam's ribs were truly on fire now, so as soon as he knew she was stable, he dropped her wrists and stepped back, turning away from her to clutch his midsection and bite the hell out of his tongue so he wouldn't break down in front of a sexy woman.

Christ almighty, that hurt.

He heard movement behind him, and when he finally caught his breath, he turned to find her sitting up on top of the armoire.

"I jump, and you steady me when I land," she said.

He nodded, too far gone with pain to argue or even think of a better way to help her.

She leaned down and put her hands on his shoulders. He caught a whiff of strawberries when she did, and his gaze shot to hers. They stayed like that for a fleeting moment. Her skin was dusty, but smooth and unblemished. He'd never seen anything like her skin—or her hair. Both were like you'd find in the pages of a magazine, not airbrushed, but real, warm, touchable.

He cleared his throat and let his gaze drift away. "Ready when you are."

The next thing he knew, she was falling through the air, and when she landed, she was on her good foot, body pressed close to his, her hands on his shoulders.

For a moment, Liam forgot about his ribs, about cops and Russians and the fact his family would be worried about him. All he could think about was that Katya was touching him, and it felt so very right.

But then he felt her turn rigid, her eyes widening in panic, and he realized he had her pinned, between him and the armoire, and she was injured, as well as fresh out of a brothel.

He stepped back and turned so she was forced to take one hand off his shoulder. Standing next to her, he said, "Are you ready to go?"

She nodded, and hopped lightly, injured foot held aloft.

They slowly made their way out of the apartment into what was left of the hallway. Liam moved them to the back stairwell of the building, listening for activity from below, signs that the rescue teams were coming their direction. He guessed they wanted to make sure the building was stable before entering, so it was taking them longer than normal.

As they made their way down the backstairs, Katya using the banister to hop, he felt in his pockets for his phone. Nothing. He didn't know what had happened to the guard who'd been stationed outside his door, but since no one had been looking for him, he guessed the guy was dead.

It was a long six floors down, and as they passed the doors opening to other floors, he could hear rescue crews moving through evacuating anyone still in the building. Finally, they reached the exit in the underground parking lot. He opened the door a crack and was relieved to find the rescuers hadn't driven into the structure. Again, probably concerned about the whole building collapsing.

"Stay here," he instructed as they moved into the parking garage. He pointed to a darkened corner near the door they'd used, and she complied with a look of relief, sitting gingerly on the curbing there.

He began a search of nearby cars, checking doors, peering in windows. Midway through the second row, he discovered a cell phone that had been left in a parked car. He noticed the red light flashing, indicating the newish Audi had an alarm system armed.

Liam listened to the commotion outside, the sirens of more police, fire, and ambulances pulling up. He looked again at that flashing red light inside the Audi's window, then made his move. He stepped back, took a deep breath, and kicked out, his boot slamming into the glass of the side window, shattering it so it bowed, hanging like a cracked curtain in the window opening.

He collapsed for a moment against the side of the car, breathing hard, his ribs screaming their disapproval as the car alarm began blaring. With all the commotion outside, Liam was counting on no one noticing or investigating the noise. It was a gamble, but he didn't have much choice.

He stood and pushed on the glass until the entire crackled sheet fell in, landing on the driver's seat. Then he reached in and grabbed the phone. He quickly made his way back to Katya, helping her stand and putting her arm around his neck as he steered her to the ramp that led out of the garage.

It took nearly fifteen minutes to scoot along the darkened wall of the garage ramp until they were outside, screened by some bushes that landscaped the exterior of the building. Beyond the plantings, a few dozen cops, paramedics, and firefighters worked to secure the building, care for the injured, and try to figure out what the hell had happened.

Katya sat on the ground, her face full of a fear he hoped never to see there again. He took the phone and sighed in relief that it didn't have a security code programmed. He shook his head. It figured that someone who was so lax they'd leave the damn thing in the car also wouldn't have it secured.

After pressing in Cian's number, he waited with a pounding heart until his brother answered.

"Yes?"

"It's me," he said.

"Jesus." Then there was no sound for a moment, and when Cian spoke again, his voice was so thick, it nearly undid Liam as well. "Where are you? Are you hurt?"

"Some cracked ribs, and our friend has a sprained or broken ankle. But we made it outside on our own. There's damn cops everywhere, though."

Cian spoke to whoever was with him for a moment, then came back on the line. "Give us a minute, we're checking on something…"

Liam gave Katya what he hoped was a reassuring smile, but she was too far gone and just stared back at him, glassy-eyed.

"Okay," Cian said. "We have one of Pop's guys in the CPD there. Tell us where you are, and he'll come to you and get you out. Badge will read O'Brian."

"Got it." Liam closed his eyes for a moment. "We're next to the parking structure ramp on the east side of the building."

"He's on the way."

"Thanks."

"Liam?"

"Yeah?"

"I thought I'd lost you," Cian said roughly.

"I know." Liam felt like a total asshole. He'd never meant to add more garbage to his brother's plate. "But you didn't, and now we know. I'll be more careful. We'll figure it out."

"This is only the beginning."

"I'm going to find a way to end it," Liam promised. "And I'll see you soon."

They disconnected the call, and it was only a few minutes later that Officer O'Brian found them and escorted them to his patrol car. They were safe, but only for now.

Chapter Nine

"How are they?" Cian asked Dr. O'Reilly as he came into the living room of the safe house.

"*They're* just fine," Liam muttered, following closely behind the doctor, shirt off and ribs taped tightly.

Dr. O'Reilly raised an eyebrow at Cian as if to say, *Can you control him?*

"Shouldn't you be in bed or something?" Cian asked from where he leaned against the back of a sofa.

"He should," the doctor scolded. "Especially since he wouldn't let me give him any painkillers."

"What the hell?" Cian held his hands up in the universal sign of frustration. "You're not going to get better if you're in pain all the time. And yes, they can find you here too, but it's going to take them a while. You know that. We have this property locked down so tight, you have at least forty-eight safe hours. You need to use them to recover."

Liam walked around Cian and sat down gingerly. Cian and the doctor followed.

"Katya has a concussion in addition to the sprained ankle." Liam winced as he adjusted his seat. "She needs to rest—no light, no screens, nothing but sleep and quiet for as long as we can get it for her. I'm not going to be out of it on painkillers when she's in that condition." His voice was firm, and Cian sighed. When his brother got like this, there was no reasoning with him. Liam was as stubborn as their father. It could be a good thing, and it could be a real pain in the ass.

The door opened, and Finn walked in, his face tense in a way it rarely was. As the family brain, the family fixer, and the son of least interest to Robbie, Finn had the most even temperament of any of the MacFarlanes. In fact, it was safe to say he had the temperament of a Milligan, his mother's side of the family. They were politicians and church patrons, not mobsters.

"Jesus, Mary, and Joseph," Finn spat as he ground to a halt in front of Liam. Cian sat back in the corner of the sofa and watched the show unfold.

"My apartment went boom," Liam snarked. Finn's face grew red, and he clenched his fists.

"You scared the hell out of us." Finn's voice was shaky and rough.

Liam shifted, his cavalier expression faltering for just a moment. "But I'm fine. The Russians are all bark—they don't have what it takes to really get me."

Finn thrust a hand into his floppy brown hair, his green eyes widening as he growled in frustration and stomped across the room, ending up staring out the window.

Cian looked at Liam, who shrugged. *Come on,* Cian mouthed. Liam sighed and rolled his eyes, then stood awkwardly.

Dr. O'Reilly motioned toward the door, and Cian nodded as the man left.

Liam stood behind Finn and spoke quietly. "I'm sorry. I know you both wanted me to get the hell out of that apartment, and I should have listened to you. But I am fine, and I'll do the careful thing from here on out."

Finn's back moved as he breathed faster than normal. Finally, Liam put a big, heavy hand on Finn's shoulder. He squeezed as he murmured, "I'm okay. We're all okay."

Cian's heart clenched as he watched the two men across the room. Liam and Finn, while next to each other in birth order, were also the most different of the four brothers, almost as though they were two halves of a whole that had been split somehow years ago. Liam was the enforcer, while Finn was the fixer, cleaning up after Liam had done his work, or finding alternate solutions when Liam's methods didn't achieve the results they needed. Where Liam was brawn, Finn was brains, and logically, they ought to be as far apart as two brothers could be. But like those two halves cleaved, Finn and Liam had a unique understanding of one another.

Finn still faced away. Liam gave one more squeeze to his brother's shoulder, then turned to Cian. "We have any whiskey in this place?"

Cian chuckled. "You think Pop would have a safe house without it?" He made his way to the galley kitchen and poured three tumblers full of Connemara. Food in the place was all nonperishable, and the accommodations were sparse, but Robbie MacFarlane made sure his safe houses always had whiskey, guns, and cash.

When Cian returned to the living room, Finn seemed recovered, feet kicked up on the coffee table, a grin on his face as he watched Liam struggle to get comfortable with his ribs bandaged.

Cian passed the glasses around and took a seat near Liam. Raising his glass, he looked at each brother in turn. "To Connor not being here," he said seriously. Both Liam and Finn nodded, relief filtering between the three of them. After they'd all had a drink, Cian got down to business.

"Lila is spending the day going over all our cybersecurity, making sure everything's as tight as possible. Then she'll make the first strike against the Russians."

"They'll be expecting something after this mess today," Liam said.

"They'll be expecting guns," Finn spoke confidently. "It's natural to fight fire with fire, like with like. They'll be surprised when it's their bank accounts we hit, and more than that, it'll take them twenty-four hours to realize we've done it, so they'll be on edge waiting for something that's not coming."

"But they're not going to quit coming after me. I humiliated Sergei when I took Katya. He's out for blood."

"Which is why we're going to keep you moving. Every twenty-four to thirty-six hours," Cian answered. "We'll rotate you, I have three properties set up already, and we'll put more in the mix if we need them."

"How long can he keep that up, though?" Finn

asked. "Cyberwars can be long."

"Plus Pop isn't going to stand for me running like a coward," Liam added, his voice gruff. "He'll want guns against the Russians if it's more than a week. He has no patience for this kind of subtle shit."

Cian ground his teeth. Robbie had no patience for anything other than bullying everyone and everything to bend to his will. Cian had infinite patience when it came to saving the lives of his brothers and trusted employees.

"Even Pop knows we can't take on the Russians like that. But you're right, he's not going to like you being on the run."

They all looked at one another, and while Cian knew it was up to him to have an answer, the adrenaline from Liam's near miss had finally caught up with him. He was exhausted—mentally and physically—and he didn't have any answers right now. All he had were questions and problems and the beginning of what he knew was going to be a hell of a headache.

"The Russians blowing up Liam's place is bound to get the cops and the feds up in arms," Finn said. "Maybe we can tell Pop, Liam has to lay low to avoid the police? It's not a lie, it's something he can understand, and it buys us some time. If we can show him how we're hacking the Russians, he'll know we're fighting back as well as playing it under the radar with the cops."

Cian nodded. It was logical—when was Finn ever not—and it would buy them some time. Maybe a week or a little longer. In the meantime, Lila had to keep hitting the Russians electronically hard and fast so they'd be more willing to negotiate when the time seemed right.

"Okay," he acquiesced, looking to Liam, who nodded as well. "We'll play the cop angle, we'll move Liam and the girl every day and a half, we'll hit the Russians with cyber strikes round the clock, and we'll present it all to Pop to postpone his frustrations."

"And when the cops really do come looking for Liam?"

"We'll tell them he's on vacation. He wasn't there when it exploded. If they want to speak to him via phone, they can do that."

"I'll get the lawyers on it ASAP," Finn said. "We'll make them work for anything."

"And I'll have Lila get a phony plane ticket and hotel room booked under Liam's name so it looks like he's off enjoying himself somewhere."

"What about the girl?" Finn asked quietly, his gaze darting to the short hallway that led to the bedroom.

"What about her?" Liam asked, his whole body tensing up.

Jesus. Cian wondered why he hadn't seen it before. Liam had a thing for the woman. Now *that* was a clusterfuck of epic proportions.

"We have to do something with her at some point," Cian told him gently. "She'll never be safe here, you know that, plus she's a liability to you. You can't take care of yourself as well if you're weighed down by her. You need to decide where you're going to send her and be done with it."

He saw it in his brother's eyes, the tenuous desperation, the beginning of rebellion. But Liam shut it down before saying, "Yeah, okay. Give us a couple of days so she gets over the concussion. I'll ask her if she has anywhere she can go, and if not, we'll just set something up for her—an ID, a ticket out of the country, a few thousand dollars."

Cian just nodded, catching Finn's gaze at the same time. Yeah, both of them could see it. Liam had something mixed up inside, Cian could only hope it wasn't too far along, because there was no way he could let his brother keep the woman. If the Russians thought she and Liam were living some sort of happily ever after, they'd make it their prime purpose in life to destroy the both of them. And there was no way Cian was going to let a woman be the death of his brother.

**

"Please tell me he's okay," Cian's mother said as she met him at the back door to the family kitchen.

"Yes, a little bruised up, but he's fine. I promise."

Angela moved across the room. "Come on, then. What do you want to eat?"

Cian smiled to himself. Like most of the world's mothers, Angela defaulted to feeding her children when she worried about them.

"I'm fine, Ma, really. But I have to talk to Pop. Is he in his study?"

Angela put a hand on his arm as he went to move past her. "Shouldn't you wait until Finn comes?"

"Finn is busy with other things." He saw the worry in her face, and it stabbed him with guilt.

"He's not in a good place," she told him, referring to his father's mood. "I know how you two get."

Irritation replaced Cian's guilt immediately. His mother's ability to minimize the violence between him and his father was astounding. The love had been lost between the two men years ago, and she damn well knew it.

"It'll be fine, Ma. Don't I always make sure of it?"

He saw the pain flash across Angela's face before she answered, "Yes, of course. He's in the study. Stop by before you leave. I have things to send for all you boys."

He brushed a quick kiss across her cheek and moved out into the hallway. Before entering his father's study, he stopped and took a deep breath, reminding himself that Robbie MacFarlane was nothing more than a vicious, bitter old man.

"Took you long enough," Robbie snapped when Cian entered. "I want to know what the hell's going on, and what the hell we're doing about it."

Cian sat in one of the large armchairs facing his father's desk and stared at the old man coldly. "Your son is fine, by the way."

"That's because he's strong," Robbie snarled. "The strongest of all my boys." Robbie raised an eyebrow in challenge to Cian. But he had stopped taking his father's bait a very long time ago.

"I've put Liam and the girl in one of our safe houses. We have to keep him out of sight of the cops. Our next step is to hit the Russians with computers. Their bank accounts, their utilities, their communications. We can't beat them gun for gun, but we can with technology."

Robbie's color heightened, as it always did when his rage took over. Robbie's response to a threat was to shoot first and think about it later. Now it was Cian's job to convince him otherwise.

"Those bastards blow up your brother's home with him in it, and your response is to turn off their lights?"

"You read the newspaper. You heard what the Russians did with the presidential election, right? It's called cyberwar, and it works. We have one of the world's best hackers on our team. She can take their money, she can interrupt their commerce, she can drive them crazy blacking out their communications. Guns will mean they send more guns. You know they have more men than we do. It's suicide. But we can make their lives hell just by letting Lila do her thing. This is how the game is played now. I know you don't like my approach most of the time, but unless you want to lose entirely, you'll let me do this."

The muscles in Robbie's jaw flexed. His anger was palpable, his frustration like a third being in the room.

"And what the hell will Liam be doing during all this?"

"We'll keep him in a safe house just until we've made a couple of strikes, then we can give the girl an airline ticket, and Liam can get back to business."

"I want the girl gone," Robbie commanded. "Your brother can find another whore to fuck. There's no way in hell she was worth all this."

"He took her for the information. We explained that. He's not fucking her. Give him a little more credit than that."

Robbie's fist clenched on the desktop, and Cian knew if the chunk of wood weren't between them, he'd be on the receiving end of one of his father's famous punches.

"I'm not giving any of you much credit these days. You're sloppy and lazy and scared. I guess that's what happens when you grow up with too much. If you'd had to work for it like I did, maybe you'd be better men."

Ice flooded Cian's veins. Robbie's insults no longer stung, they merely added another layer to the armor he wore day in and day out. A steel so thick, he could withstand anything Robbie might hurl at him.

"Be that as it may, we're all you've got. Tell Ma I had to run. She can feed me next time." He stood and walked out of his father's house.

**

It was midnight when Cian arrived at the small park that fronted a portion of the Chicago river outside of downtown. The texts had been pinging on his phone for the last four hours, and his patience was worn beyond thin.

He stepped away from the light provided by the one overhead near the picnic tables and made his way to the edge of the grass where the bank rolled down to the dark water. A cool breeze drifted up from the surface of the river, and he realized he was sweating beneath his short-sleeved button-down. Sometimes he wondered how much stress a man's thirty-four-year-old body could take before he stroked out or dropped dead from his heart exploding. If he had many more days like today, he'd probably get the answer to that question soon.

"You finally pissed Don off so much, you're stuck with me," Bruce said as he slid up alongside

Cian, a cigarette dangling from one hand.

Cian stepped away from Bruce. "You know they made those e-cigs so you don't have to poison the rest of us with your secondhand smoke."

The federal agent muttered something less than polite but dropped the butt on the ground and crushed it beneath his dress shoe heel.

"So start talking." Bruce's voice was weary. Cian was willing to bet the fed had been living through a hell of a day as well. Not that he gave a shit. Bruce dropping dead from the stress would only make Cian's life easier—at least for a while.

"You knew the Russians were in town," he answered as nonchalantly as possible.

"Yeah, and we figured they'd be pushing your borders, but we didn't think things would escalate quite this fast. What the hell did you do?"

"It's possible we took something they *thought* belonged to them."

"Fuck." Bruce spat on the ground before shoving his hands in the front pockets of his very unstylish slacks. "I thought you were trying to keep your brothers alive and out of prison. Stealing from the Russians sounds like a one-way ticket to the morgue."

The water lapped quietly against the shore, and Cian breathed deeply, wondering what it would feel like to slip beneath the cold surface and let nature take over. Quiet. Cool. Numb. What a relief it would be to just let go once and for all. Turn his back on all of it—on all of them—and rest. Really rest.

He cleared his throat as he tried to clear the thoughts, because, tempting as they might be, he couldn't, and he knew it.

"What we took didn't belong to the Russians. It was something they should never have had in the first place. Trust me, we were the good guys here, but they're pissed, and they'll use it as an excuse to go scorched earth."

"Well, on behalf of the people of Chicago, I'd like to thank you. Scorched earth will undoubtedly take out more civilians like the woman who died in the apartment explosion today."

Cian sighed deeply. He felt sorry for the life lost, but in the midst of his current battles, he didn't have time to focus on her or anyone other than his nearest and dearest.

"You got me here. What do you want to know?"

Bruce stepped closer, his voice dropping even as it grew more venomous. "We want to fucking know how to end the Russians. It's not rocket science, MacFarlane."

"Apparently, it is, since the Bratva have been in the States for decades and you haven't been able to stop them yet. You've had all that time to figure this out while they've been living off America's weaknesses for drugs and sex. Either it's exactly that hard or the government's exactly that stupid."

Cian could feel the other man's anger rolling off him, but Bruce had come without backup, so he wouldn't be lunging at Cian tonight. Bruce might be a wild hair away from doing something stupid most days, but he didn't actually want to die.

The fed released a long shuddering breath, and Cian laughed bitterly in the dark. "Good choice," he muttered.

"Give us something, MacFarlane," Bruce ground out. "Or we'll tell the locals to look harder for Liam.

You know it's only a matter of hours before they find out that apartment was his. They're going to want to talk to him. I can make that go away or I can ramp it up. Your choice."

"I gave you the address of the brothel they're running. I'm not sure what else you think I know."

"We've been watching it, but we already know we won't be able to tie it to anyone. If we raid, we'll get a handful of low-level soldiers who can't tell us anything about the organization. They say 'da' when told to shoot, that's about it." He paused. "But you're going to answer what happened today. How? When? Where? If you'll coordinate with us, I'll make sure none of your men are taken in when the bullets stop flying."

Cian snorted in disdain. "You really think we're that stupid? That we'd go at the Bratva with guns? I don't have that kind of firepower, and you know it. They have endless soldiers to send in from New York. My entire crew would be wiped out inside a week."

"There's no way in hell your daddy is going to let them blow up Liam's apartment building and not answer."

Cian grunted. "We have other plans."

"I'm waiting."

"What do I get for it?" he asked. This was the first chance he'd had in months to get ahead of the feds. The cyberwar Lila was launching would put them in possession of a lot of valuable information about the Russians' business—account numbers, names, addresses, transactions. He could trade that. He could get some of the heat off his own family and his brothers.

"Not a damn thing," Bruce huffed in indignation. "You're the one with shit to lose here. You seem to keep forgetting that."

If only, Cian thought.

He took his hands out of his front pants pockets and started to jingle the car keys. "Well, it was nice talking to you, Agent. See you around."

He got only a few steps before Bruce's voice sliced through the darkness. "A three-month reprieve."

Cian stopped, turning back even though he could barely see the other man's outline in the darkness.

"Reprieve from what?"

"From giving us info on your own operations."

Cian didn't smile, though he wanted to.

"The fact is, the Bratva are bigger fish than you, and if we can get ahold of them, it'll take all our time and resources to do it. Don't go thinking we won't still want to snack on the Devils when we're done feasting on vodka, but we can postpone it. You can have a little breathing space while you're helping us grab the Russians."

Inside, Cian was rejoicing. Outside, he kept up appearances. "And I'm supposed to thank you for this?"

"You're supposed to remember that we let Connor go. You owe us for that."

"Fine, three months, no more questions about MacFarlane operations, and I give you whatever we find on the Russians."

"Okay, start now."

"We're fighting back with cyber. We'll be hacking into their accounts, their records, fucking with their systems. I'll hand you everything we find while we do it."

"Who do you have in your shop with that know-how?"

Cian's blood pressure shot sky-high, and he clenched his fists at his sides to keep from sending one flying at Bruce's pudgy nose.

"None of your business," he gritted. "You'll get all the information. That's the part that matters to you."

"Whatever you say." Bruce sounded smug, and Cian was glad he couldn't see the man's face.

He turned on his heel, tossing off, "I'll be in touch," as he strode away back to the parking lot. Every step matched the aching pain in his chest and the waves of nausea rolling through him. How much longer could he protect Lila from the feds? Rogue was his ace in the hole, the last bit of valuable information he could use to secure safety for Liam and Finn. But would he be able to do it when the time came?

Because right now, the idea of betraying Lila made him want to vomit up his very soul.

Chapter Ten

The string of code seemed to go on forever. Lila had hacked everything from Credit Suisse to the FBI, but never had she seen a system this complex. She had to hand it to them, the Russians were good.

"You're telling me you can't get in?" Cian asked, his brow furrowed in concern.

Lila ground her teeth. "I can get in. It's just going to take a while."

"How long is a while?"

She turned and glanced at him where he stood near her living room desk. "Hours. Possibly a couple of days."

"Is there something else we can hit them with in the meantime?" He paused, looking stressed to her eyes, though he did a damn good job of trying to hide it.

"Yes. There are other places I can hit, but it will take me away from this. If you want the big strike, you have to be patient. If you want smaller ones in the meantime, it'll delay the bigger one."

He snapped then. "Goddammit!" he spat as he pounded the side of his fist against the nearest wall. She didn't point out that he'd just dented the wallboard. He was paying her enough she could get it fixed. Hell, he was paying her enough she could buy the whole town house in cash ten times over. Money was really wasted on Lila. The only things she ever bought with it were more bracelets and computer hardware.

She glanced at the screen again. It was a puzzle, and she'd never yet met a puzzle she couldn't solve, but some took longer than others. This one was going to take a while.

"There's one other possibility," she said tentatively.

"That's good." He pulled over a chair, sitting, and gave her his full attention. Cian MacFarlane's full attention could set a girl's heart to beating faster. "I need another possibility."

She chewed her bottom lip for a moment. Cian's situation was precarious—always. And he stayed alive by keeping his circle tight, and small. The fewer people who knew his business, the safer he was. He wasn't going to like her idea, but in her opinion it was his only option.

"I have a friend—"

"No." His response was fast and sharp.

She raised an eyebrow at him.

"We can't involve unknowns. You realize that, surely. This is far too dangerous and sensitive."

"My friend is the best, almost as good as me." She let one side of her mouth lift in a smug smile. Cian softened just a touch. "If I can bring in

Scotchboy, he can help me by hitting the lesser targets while I work on this one."

"Scotchboy?"

"His handle," she explained patiently.

"So who is this guy?"

"I don't know that it *is* a guy, but most likely, it is."

"You don't even know their gender, but you're willing to trust them with our cyberwar? You're willing to risk them giving information to the Russians or the feds or Interpol?"

She shook her head. "There's a risk, but it's small. I've known Scotchboy for years, and even though we don't talk as much anymore, I trust him—her—them."

Cian's lips pressed together tightly, and his jaw was like stone.

"I won't tell him what we're doing, just give him a list of sites we need to gain access to. He'll work on them, and once he's a step or two from breaking in, he'll give me the code, and I'll do the actual penetration. It wouldn't work with just anyone, but he thinks a lot like I do. I know I'll be able to understand the direction he takes and finish off his process."

"I don't like it—"

"I know you don't," she said calmly, "but there is only one of me. I've hired on more eyes at Rogue to keep tabs on the day-to-day, but you only allow *me* to monitor your accounts, and then I'm running a war to boot. I'm a badass, but Cian, I'm only one badass."

He gave her a guilty smile. "Okay. I get it. I've asked too much."

"I can handle it, but you have to *let* me handle it. I'm running a business now, and serving as your

CTO, so to speak. I can do it, but I have to be able to outsource as needed."

He looked at the floor for a moment. "You're amazing. You know that, right? And I'm sorry. I tell you I'll give you anything you need, then I try to keep you confined with all sorts of rules at the same time."

"You're not used to trusting anyone but your brothers," she said plainly.

He chuckled quietly. "No, I'm not." Then he pinned her with his blue-eyed gaze. "But I trust you, and if you say this Scotchboy person can help, then we should bring him…her…*them* in. I'll stop micromanaging. You do what you need to."

She smiled then, because it meant the world that Cian trusted her. He had everything to lose, and she would never put him or his family at risk.

"Okay, then. I'll contact Scotch, and we'll get the small stuff started right away. I'm guessing we can have the lights and water shut off at that brothel within the next twelve hours. Utilities should have the strongest security, but all too often, they're disappointingly easy to crack."

He grinned at her. "You love this stuff, don't you?"

She shrugged, trying not to let him know how right he was. "I like a challenge. These overseas accounts are definitely challenging."

Cian stood and stretched. "I'd better let you get back to it, then," he said, leaning down and giving her a brotherly peck on the cheek. They were apparently not lovers today. But not just business partners either. More like friends. Or siblings. Lila was never sure, and it was starting to make her crazy.

She thought she could handle it either way—or

she'd learn to—as long as she knew. If he wanted her to leave for good, she'd do it, and survive. If he wanted to really try, take a leap at something for the long term, then she'd be right there with him. What was making her nuts was the in-between. Because little by little, Cian was capturing her heart at the same time he'd hung a guillotine over her head.

He walked to her door and paused, turning to look at her over his shoulder. "One more thing…"

She waited, the sound of a car horn blaring from outside her living room window.

"I'll need you to save all the information you get on their accounts, financials, any security footage you tap into. Put it all on USB drives for me."

She narrowed her eyes at him. "Oh-kay…" But before she could ask more, the door was open and he was walking out, leaving Lila to wonder what Cian wasn't telling her, and why it hurt that he wasn't.

**

Katya woke with a start, light piercing her eyelids with tiny needles that stabbed at her temples.

"Is that too bright?" a man's voice asked.

For a moment, her heart raced and she panicked, visions of a hand fitting over her mouth, making it impossible to scream and nearly impossible to breathe. Then he spoke again. "Here, I brought you something. Let me help you sit up."

She pried open one eye and looked into the face of Liam MacFarlane. He was big, and looming over the bed, he looked even bigger, but in spite of that, in spite of the rugged scruff on his jaw and chin, and the muscles that bulged in his arms, neck, and shoulders, in spite of the fact he was a criminal, Katya realized she was no longer afraid of him.

He smiled gently at her and carefully extended an arm. "Can I help?" he asked. "You got a concussion in the explosion. Doc says you should take it really easy for at least a couple of days."

She nodded, and as he helped her scoot up to sit against the backboard, she suddenly realized she probably looked like hell.

She ran fingers through her hair, finding it full of snarls. Meanwhile, her teeth were covered in fuzz and her eyes were nearly glued shut.

Liam pulled a folding chair over near the bed and picked up a mug from the nightstand. "Here's some coffee. I made it strong the way you liked it the other day, but I can put sugar in it if you want. There's also tea. Would that be better?"

He seemed almost nervous, and Katya swallowed, feeling oddly unsettled with him so close. Not scared. Just sort of fluttery. Like she used to get when she had a crush on a boy in school. But she was far beyond crushes. Maybe a few weeks ago, before she'd come to America, but no longer. She'd seen what lay beneath the surface of men. She'd vowed never to *flutter* for one again.

"Coffee is good. Thank you," she replied as she took the warm cup from him.

"I'm sorry to wake you, but you've been sleeping most of the last fifteen hours, and it's possible we may have to leave here at some point soon. I wanted you to have a chance to shower and eat. Does your head hurt?"

She did an internal assessment for a moment before answering. "No. My ears are…humming?" She made a little motion next to her left ear.

"Ringing, maybe? Mine have been since the explosion. It's getting less, but the doctor said it would take a while to wear off."

"Yes. That. Ringing."

"How do you feel otherwise?"

She shrugged as she took a sip of the coffee, amazed he could make it so delicious. "I think okay. Ankle hurts, but not too much."

He let out a small breath and leaned back in the chair. "Good. That's good to hear. You should still take it easy, stay in bed, keep the lights low as long as possible. When it's time to go, we'll have to move fast."

She sipped more coffee thoughtfully. "What happen now? We move...how many times? How long? They will not stop coming."

Liam crossed his arms over his chest as he leaned back. She saw the mask that slid across his face when he talked about business.

"We won't have to keep running," Liam growled. "My brothers and I are not about to let the Russians beat us. We'll get them, and we'll make sure you're safe, no matter what."

Katya was surprised at the vehemence in his voice. She knew he was a hard man; he was a mobster. She knew he was a fearless man. He'd taken her from the Russian whorehouse. But the man she'd seen for the last few days had been kind, considerate, almost gentle. That was the man she was beginning to feel she knew. However, given what she'd learned about men in general over the last few weeks, she couldn't ignore the parts of Liam that she hadn't been seeing.

He was a criminal, plain and simple. He did bad things to people, he hurt them, he used them, he was dangerous, even if not to her.

"Why do you do this?" she asked suddenly. "I give you all the information, I'm no use to you anymore. I must be...how do you say? A weakness?"

"A liability," Liam corrected.

"Yes. A liability. Why keep me when I am only liability?"

Liam's eyes grew dark, and he cleared his throat, looking almost uncomfortable. Katya watched him warily, wondering what he was thinking, feeling. She firmly believed he felt and thought much more than most people realized.

"I left you that night," he said finally. "The first time I found you when they had you taped to the chair? I left you."

She remembered it well.

"In my line of work, I do things that aren't good, things that hurt people, but until that night, I'd never felt guilt for any of it. After I left that room, after I left that house, I realized leaving you was the worst thing I'd ever done."

She stared at him, almost disbelieving. "You kill men, no?"

He gave her a look that said he wasn't going to answer that question, but that same look gave her all the answer she needed.

"How could leaving me feel worse than killing?"

He scratched his head, a wry smile sliding across his lips. "The people I deal with in my job, they chose to be there. They knew the rules, they knew the risks, they're willing participants. And while I feel sorry for their families, that's between them and the people they love. You didn't choose this. You didn't choose to be kidnapped. You didn't choose to be used or beaten. You didn't choose this life."

She felt those damn tears burning behind her eyes again, and this time, she wasn't sure if she could keep them away by sheer will.

"Many years ago, my brother was forced to do something he didn't choose. It changed him and it changed *me* forever. I understand what it means to have your choices taken from you. And after I left you there that night, I realized this was a chance. A chance for me to give someone back their choice. I want to give you back your choice. I want to help you in whatever you decide to do from here."

And that was when the dam broke.

Katya gave one gut-wrenching sob before she pulled it all back inside, tight in a knot in her center where she held on to it with everything she had, because she feared if she let it go, she would never be able to pull the pieces together again.

She put a hand over her eyes, trying to cover her shame. Then she felt Liam's skin on hers, warm and rough. He gently pried her hand from her face and looked at her as tears rolled down her cheeks.

"Don't be ashamed," he told her fiercely. "Don't be ashamed to let me see what it feels like. I've known a lot of men in my life—men who do horrific things, men who are big and tough and scare others— but I have never known anyone as strong as you. If you need to cry, you cry. If you need to yell, you yell. And if you need me, I will be here to make sure you always have a choice."

As Katya gave in to it, she fell into his arms, sobbing. He held her gently and stroked her hair, and for the first time since she'd been shoved in the back of that van, she felt hope.

**

The Russians were demanding a meeting with Xavier, and Lila felt like she'd swallowed a lead balloon.

I need to see you right away, she texted Cian as she opened the door to her row house and stepped inside, shutting it firmly in the face of the guard that Cian kept on her at all times.

It was nearly ten minutes before Cian texted her back.

What's wrong?

Need to talk in person.

Meet me at Starbucks in one hour, came his reply.

She paced up and down the length of her small living room, glancing every few moments at the message she'd received from the Russians nearly ninety minutes ago. It demanded a meeting, *very soon,* it had stipulated.

Since the day she'd fed the Russians information about Cian being alone at his boxing gym, Sergei hadn't asked for anything. The way Lila figured it, the Russians had been distracted by setting up their brothel, so they hadn't been thinking much about Xavier.

But now that an all-out war between the Bratva and the MacFarlanes was gearing up, they'd circled back around, wanting Xavier to give them whatever information he could, suspecting he might be double-dealing with the MacFarlanes and probably preparing to eliminate him because of it.

Lila also knew as soon as the Russians realized

someone had beaten them to it and Xavier was already dead, they would come after Rogue, and they would come after it hard. She could leave, disappear, dump Rogue, let it all play on without her. Her mother was recovering from the surgery; her treatment was over. If Lila had to, she could go now. But something strange had happened in the weeks she'd been managing the dark website. It had started to feel like hers. And right now, at this point in her life, there was virtually nothing else that did.

Lila's father was most likely dead, and while the cancer treatment had gone well, Lila knew deep down that her mother might not be in this world much longer. Cian seemed to be temporary as well, since he showed no signs of asking for something longer term. Rogue was the only thing she had that was truly hers, that she could control, that she had a say over. The idea of walking away and letting the Russians destroy it didn't sit well.

An hour later, Lila slid into a chair across the table from Cian at their Starbucks. He was in his standard business-casual attire—a moss-green short-sleeved button-down shirt that molded to the planes of his chest, untucked, with flat-fronted dark slacks. His hair was messy, his eyes tired, and more than anything, she wanted to reach out and just hold him until that tortured look had left him for good.

He reached across the table and held her hand in his. She stifled the ache that swelled in her heart. Every time he touched her, every time he spoke to her in the dark, every time his body covered hers, she knew she gave another piece of herself to him, pieces she could never get back.

"What's happened?" he asked, concern etching

his words.

"The Russians want a meeting with Xavier." She glanced around to make sure no one could hear their conversation.

"I wish I could say I'm surprised, but I figured this was coming. We're in a war now, and they're going to insist on using every advantage they have. They're going to want to meet face-to-face with Xavier in order to impress upon him what will happen if he doesn't give them what they want."

Lila's heart beat a little quicker at that.

"All you can do is quit communicating with them. We haven't gotten much useful out of them in days anyway."

"If I cut them off, they'll come after Rogue." She wondered how Cian could be so cavalier about the potential for damage here.

"Don't worry. Even if they come after it, they don't know about you. They'll be looking for Xavier. Once they've figured out he's vanished, it won't matter."

"They'll destroy Rogue, though," she repeated. "If they can't find Xavier, they'll start hunting for it and they won't stop until they tear it down. And if they can't do it themselves they'll give the feds information they find, especially since they know the MacFarlanes are doing business there."

Cian looked at her grimly. "And as much as I hate to lose the family the income, it might be time to shut Rogue down anyway."

Something in Lila rebelled at that. It was *hers*. Xavier might have started it and she may have acquired it by some pretty dark dealings, but Rogue was hers.

"No." Her words sliced through the air between them.

Cian's eyes widened. He didn't get told no often, and he'd never been told no by her.

"Look, I understand you've worked hard there, but this has been coming. You've known you need to leave. You can get out of town and let us handle whatever happens to Rogue."

"There has to be another way. Rogue is doing better than ever. It's earning you money, it's earning a lot of people money, and I'm not ready to shut it down."

Cian leaned back in his chair and crossed his arms. The look on his face said he wasn't going to budge. But Lila's mind started spinning out the possibilities.

"Never in any of the communications I've seen between Xavier and the Russians did it say they had met him in person," she pressed. "I don't think they've ever seen him, I don't think they've ever spoken to him on the phone."

"But you don't *know* that."

"Not for certain, but pretty damn close."

He shook his head, his mouth in a grim line, jaw tensed. "I don't like where you're going with this."

"It's perfectly believable that I would have an alias I operated under, that I would choose to be a man online. Especially when dealing with people like the Bratva."

"Uh-uh. No. Way." He sat forward, arms on the table. His voice was low so no one would overhear, but his tone brooked no argument.

"You will *not* meet with the Russians, Lila."

She felt heat climb into her cheeks as anger

bubbled up in her chest. "Why not?" she snapped back.

"You have no idea what they're like," he answered sharply. "They do not take kindly to being duped. They do not take kindly to being denied. You may think you have an idea of what they're capable of, but you don't."

"I can do this." A thread of steel ran through her words. "I can meet with them, I can feed them information that we decide on, and I can keep Rogue in business."

"Over my dead body."

"No," she snapped back, "You'll shut down Rogue over mine."

Chapter Eleven

Cian stared at Lila in shock. He couldn't believe what he was hearing. This was Lila—smart, savvy, sweet Lila. Lila was brilliant, but Lila lived behind a screen. She might crawl all over the dark web, but she didn't do anything like that in real life.

Hell, as long as Cian had known Lila, she'd been so very normal in how she lived. He'd had to force her to learn how to defend herself and shoot a gun, and he still wasn't sure if she carried it like he'd told her to. Now suddenly, she wanted to meet with a Russian mob boss? Had she lost her mind?

"Have you lost your mind?"

"No more than the rest of you," Lila replied, eyes flashing. "You and your family got me into this. That doesn't mean that you get to decide how I get out."

He sat back in his seat, more than a little shocked by both her tone and her words. While Cian knew he and his family bore some of the responsibility for the predicament Lila found herself in, he'd also done everything in his power to protect her and keep her out of the line of fire. She'd never blamed him, never accused him, never seemed to harbor any ill will toward him. But now, here it was.

"I had no idea you felt that way."

The spark in her eyes didn't dim, but the grim line of her mouth softened somewhat. "I know you didn't get me into this life. But since I met you, things seem to get more and more complicated every day. And now that they have, now that Rogue's mine, I'm the one who gets to decide when I give it up."

Cian wasn't used to being disobeyed by anyone but his brothers. The FBI might manipulate him, the Russians might threaten him, the Mexicans might get in his way, but in his own house, in the MacFarlane organization, no one disobeyed Cian. Well, no one except Liam, Finn, and Connor.

But now this tiny slip of a woman was daring to, and what the hell was he supposed to do with that?

"Lila," he said softly. "You know I only want to keep you safe."

She continued to stare at him, and for the first time, he started to understand why she was so good at what she did. There was a tenacity there in her eyes, a stubborn patience that said she could outlast anyone or anything.

"I can't send one of my men with you if you were to meet with the Russians. There's no way for us to protect you. I don't think you realize... I couldn't bear it if something happened to you."

That mask of defiance finally slid away from her face. Her gaze gentled, and she swayed toward him even though he was across the table.

"I know you can stop me from doing this, but I

also know you respect me. I've proven my loyalty, and even without the personal stuff between us, I think you know I would never do anything to hurt you."

"It's not me I'm worried about getting hurt here," he pleaded.

"But isn't *my* safety *my* choice?"

"When I took care of things for you that day," he said with an edge to his voice, "you became one of my responsibilities. You are part of my organization, and that means you answer to me. You do what I say, when I say. You are no longer a free agent. You are a member of the Dublin Devils."

She blinked at him, and he saw the tiniest of tremors in her bottom lip. He got a knot in his core and wanted to take it all back immediately. "Lila—"

"No, it's fine. I understand. I'll start working to shut things down at Rogue. And I'd like that plane ticket you promised. Please let me know as soon as you've made the arrangements."

Before he could say another word, she stood and was moving toward the door. He sighed in frustration, running a hand through his hair, as he watched her walk away.

"So that went well," Danny said as he approached Cian's table, glancing at Lila over his shoulder.

Cian glared at his guard, who smiled back cheekily.

"Where to now, boss?"

Hell, thought Cian. Straight to hell.

**

Liam hovered over Katya as she packed her meager belongings, and Cian watched with a mixture of horror and fascination, his brow furrowed in concern. He'd never seen his brother like this. Yes, Liam had an active social life. Lots of women. He was a party on beefy legs, always up for a night out, a drink, and a quick trip to the nearest flat surface. But Liam didn't hover—especially not over a woman.

"Hey." He motioned for Liam to come outside with him.

"I'll be right outside," Liam told the willowy blonde. She smiled at him sweetly and nodded. Cian's head began to throb. This was the last thing he needed right now.

As the door to the small house closed behind them, Cian walked to the porch railing and leaned back against it.

"You're sleeping with her? Really? I mean I guess I should have predicted that one, given what she looks like, but I have to admit, you fooled me. I really thought you felt guilty for leaving her there and wanted more information on their operation."

Liam crossed his arms in front of his chest, his forehead wrinkling beneath the baseball cap he wore backward.

"I'm not sleeping with her. I *did* feel guilty for leaving her, and I *did* hope she had more information about what Sergei was doing."

Cian nodded, crossing his own arms and creating a tension so thick between them, it could probably be felt a block away. Out of the corner of his eye, he saw Danny move away down the sidewalk to give them some privacy. He tried to keep any dustups between him and his brothers private, but he was so frustrated right now, he couldn't stop himself.

"So all the doe-eyed looks in there don't mean you have a thing for her? Dammit. We don't have time for shit like this right now, Liam."

Liam scowled at the wooden floor of the porch for a moment. "I seem to remember you having plenty of time for Connor and *his* woman when they wanted to leave town together—leave the family, leave the business, leave you with their mess to clean up. I tried to get us some valuable information and now I'm staying low for a few weeks. I'm not seeing why I'm the one getting his ass chewed."

"So you do admit you're involved with her?"

"No, I'm not—not that way. She was dealt a crappy hand, man. She was kidnapped and forced to—" He swallowed and his voice broke, and Cian knew then, even if Liam didn't yet, that it was over. He hadn't thought he'd ever see the day his stubbornly loyal younger brother would turn that loyalty toward someone other than a MacFarlane. But as he watched Liam struggle with the onslaught of emotions Katya's predicament brought, he realized he might lose his biggest protector in a way he'd never dreamed.

Liam looked up at him. "I don't know everything they did to her in there." His voice was hushed now. "But you have to realize it was a nightmare. She was covered in bruises, and I could see the panic in her eyes every time I got within arm's reach of her. It's only the last couple of days she's started to trust I'm not going to hurt her. I can feel her relaxing."

Cian nodded, amazed his brother had noticed these things about Katya.

"And she's still sick worrying over her friend,"

Liam added, looking away for a moment.

"We can't save the friend," Cian warned, though it rubbed him wrong to say it.

"I know that." Liam's mouth grew tight with frustration. "Stop acting like I'm Connor. I'm not going to run off on some tangent and do something stupid."

"You grabbed Katya from the Russians," Cian reminded him. "That wasn't the height of rational thought."

Liam flipped him off, and Cian couldn't help but grin.

"Speaking of women, I'm having a little trouble with Lila."

He probably deserved Liam's smirk, but it still made Cian want to smack it off his brother's face.

"So you've come to me for some advice? It makes sense. I do fancy myself something of an expert."

"You seem to forget who taught you all those tricks in the first place."

Liam chuckled. "Yeah, I suppose that's true."

Cian ran a hand through his hair and narrowed his eyes for a moment. "The Russians are insisting on meeting with Xavier. I told Lila it's time to close up shop and for her to leave town."

"And she doesn't want to."

"How did you figure that out so fast? I sure wasn't expecting it."

"She's in charge of a very lucrative business," Liam answered. "Not a lot of people would want to give that up."

"I don't think she cares about the money, but she has gotten attached to running Rogue. Maybe it's because she doesn't have much family, maybe it's just the challenge of the work. But whatever it is, she's sunk her teeth in and doesn't want to let go."

"She can't be Xavier, so how is she proposing to deal with the Russians?"

"She wants to meet with them herself and tell them Xavier was a cover for her all along."

Liam seemed to think about it for a moment. "It could work," he said. "If none of them have ever met Xavier, who's to say he's not a she? They're computer geeks. They catfish all the time, right?"

"I think you're missing the point here. She wants to *meet* with them. Face-to-face with Sergei and his boys."

"Well, if she wants to take the chance," Liam answered lightly.

"How the hell can you say that? She has no idea what she's getting into."

"She's a grown-up, and a smart one. If anybody can handle themselves in a situation like that, it's her."

Cian raised his eyes to the ceiling, rolling his shoulders once, working hard not to explode. How could Liam not understand how Cian felt about Lila? Not realize that Cian would do almost anything to protect her, just as he protected *everyone* he loved.

Liam's voice softened a touch. "Look, I know you care about her, but I also know there's no way you can protect her twenty-four seven, and you can't keep her."

"That doesn't mean I want to send her to her death."

"She was living the life when you met her. You can admit how smart she is, but you don't think she's smart enough to make this choice?"

Cian ground his teeth at that one. Liam was right, Lila was the smartest person he'd ever known. How could he say she wasn't smart enough to understand this risk?

"I need to talk to Finn. I need him to tell me what we can get out of a meeting between Lila and the Russians."

"And that's just the kind of brainy info Finn will love to give you."

Danny approached and took a step onto the bottom stair of the porch. "Boss? We really need to get moving. Word on the street is the Russians know we're hiding Liam in this neighborhood. It's just a matter of time before they find the exact house."

Cian nodded at Liam, who headed back inside the house. A moment later, he reemerged with Katya alongside.

"We're ready," Liam said, looking warmly at the lithe blonde next to him.

Cian got that same knot in his stomach again as he watched his brother with the girl. He wondered where all this would end up. And he thought back to Liam's words to him: *you can't keep her.*

**

It was after midnight when Lila heard the knock on her door. Always a night owl, she hadn't yet gone to bed, but had to pull on some sweats with the T-shirt and underwear she'd been wearing while she read an e-book under the covers.

"Yes?" she asked through the front door.

"It's me," came Cian's voice.

She opened the door, and he stepped inside,

Danny leaned in, giving her a wry smile as he shut the door behind his boss.

"Hi," Cian said softly, staring at her.

She felt like a snarled mess inside, so happy to see him, yet angry and sad all at the same time. She tried to temper the emotions and gave him her most neutral expression.

"Can we talk?" He gestured to the living room.

She nodded, arms folded tightly across her middle, and led him to the sofa, where she took one end and he took the other.

"I'm sorry about how things went earlier. You have to know..." He rubbed the back of his neck, clearly agitated. "I care about you, Lila. And the idea of the Russians and what they could do to you, it makes me crazy."

She folded her legs up underneath herself, leaning against the arm of the sofa, too aware of his heated gaze on her as she moved.

"I understand the feeling." She gave him a hard look.

"Touché," he replied.

"And I'm not interested in dying or being used as a sex slave, but this is a calculated risk. This is what I do every day. Hacking is all about calculated risks. It's gambling..." She paused. "I'm just starting to realize that."

She closed her eyes for one brief moment and saw her father's face, and understood, at that moment, his legacy was much bigger than she'd ever imagined. While she'd always thought she was taking what her father had dragged her into and turning it against the world, what she'd really done was turn it against herself. She had become him. She might not play poker and bet at the races, but she gambled all the same.

So now she was about to take a lifetime of experience and turn it into her biggest gamble ever. One that involved more than other people's money, more than anyone's reputation, more even than possible jail time. She was going to gamble with her own life. And she felt she could win because she was smarter than her opponents. But wasn't that the fatal flaw of all gamblers?

"I'm not sure you have all the facts you need to calculate the risk on this one. The Bratva doesn't behave like the kinds of people you've been dealing with at Rogue. They don't even behave like me. They're more like an entire organization of my father," he continued.

"I've met your father. I've watched your father. I think I get the idea."

He leaned forward, elbows on his knees, and looked at her from under the shock of hair falling over his brow. "No, you don't. Even Connor and Finn don't get it. The only two people in this world who truly know what my father is capable of are Liam and me."

As many things as Cian and Lila had shared, things about his family weren't among them. She knew how much he loved his brothers. She knew he'd facilitated Connor's disappearance with Jess, but Cian didn't talk about his father, or the inner workings of his family. Lila and Cian had touched each other's bodies, and try hard as they might to avoid it, they'd touched each other's hearts, but they'd kept away from touching each other's souls.

Now, when she saw what was in Cian's eyes, Lila

felt her resolve falter. She had a simmering need to see what lay at his very core, the essence of who he was and why he did what he did.

"Tell me," she demanded before she could stop herself. "Tell me what he did."

Cian watched her, his blue eyes sparking in the low light, his expression tense with pain.

"No," she corrected, "don't. I'm sorry I asked. I shouldn't pry."

He reached across the gap between them and took her hand in his. "It's not because I don't trust you. It's because I don't want to burden you. You have a good heart, Lila. It would hurt you, and I don't want Robbie MacFarlane to ever hurt another person I care about."

She understood.

"But believe me when I say the Russians are capable of every cruelty he is and possibly more. If you insist on doing this—meeting with them—I can't promise to protect you or to save you. I'll do everything in my power—" He paused as if he was going to continue, but then swallowed the words back down. "But I can't *promise* anything."

No, she thought, Cian couldn't promise anything. And wasn't that the story of them. No promises, no future. He'd never lied to her, and she knew he wasn't now. But still, she was going to do it. And yes, she wasn't ready to give up Rogue, and yes, she hoped she could find out something that would benefit Cian, but maybe she was also going to do this because she really had nothing to lose. Because without a future with Cian, she was beginning to think she didn't really want a future at all.

"I understand," she answered. "Does this mean

you're going to let me do it? Meet with the Russians?"

His gaze went to the ceiling briefly. "God help me, I think I am."

The moment of triumph crossed over into fear in a split second. She was going to meet with the Bratva. It was a little sobering. But she rebounded quickly because she could do this. She knew she could. She could keep Rogue alive and also help Cian. It was worth it, and she was a gambler's daughter after all.

"They expected me to answer them this afternoon. I didn't. I'm sure they're very unhappy."

"That's okay. We can spin it. You've been afraid to meet with them because you've been deceiving them. It goes with the story you said you wanted to tell."

Yes, she thought, it did. It all fit. "I've been thinking more about that. In case they have ever seen Xavier or a photo of him, I think I should say he was an employee. It's possible that when they researched him in the first place, they found some photos of him, or even that they had him followed before they approached him. But if I say he was an employee who I used as the 'face' of Rogue, I think that will explain it all."

"As usual," he said, "Your idea is gold."

"Okay, so how do we proceed?"

"We get Finn over here, and we work out the entire thing from the moment you answer their demand to meet to the minute you walk away from them unharmed." His voice was fierce with determination, and Lila felt a surge of courage in her own chest.

"And I bet you're going to bring Finn over right now." She smiled.

"You'd win that bet." He pulled his phone out of his pocket and shot off a text. When it pinged in response a second later, he looked at her. "He's on the way."

"Guess I should make some coffee, then."

Cian stood when she did and put a hand on her arm to stop her.

"How much longer?" His eyes were tender.

She cocked her head as she looked at him, trying to understand what he meant.

"How much longer are you going to stay?"

She swallowed the lump that formed as his meaning became clear. How much longer meant how much longer could she manage Rogue? How much longer could she help her mother? How much longer could she pretend Cian was hers? How much longer? It was the single greatest question in her life. And the only one she didn't have an answer to.

"I don't know," she told him honestly.

"I can't protect you forever."

She watched him again, and a shard of glass wedged in her heart. Protect her from the Russians? Protect her from the world in general? Or protect her from something she didn't even know was after her yet? The look in his eyes sent a tremor down her spine.

She swallowed and nodded. "Okay. I know. Let me help with the Russians, and then I'll go."

His gaze softened, and he reached out to run a finger down her cheek. "It's not what I want, Lila. Just what has to be."

So now she knew. She had her answer, and she knew it had to be. She also knew no matter what, it wasn't going to be pretty.

Chapter Twelve

It was nearly midnight by the time Liam got Katya and their few belongings stowed in the small duplex outside of Oak Brook. It was their third safe house in one week, and Liam had to admit he was tiring of it. He wasn't sure what he had thought would happen when he took Katya in the first place. While he wasn't like Connor, who would act with no thought at all, Liam planned things on a moment-by-moment basis. In his world, life was like a military operation. You made sure to be prepared before you went in. But you didn't look beyond the next mission, the next twenty-four hours, because really, you didn't know if you would be alive for it.

So, Liam had known he wanted to save her, and known he was compelled to protect her, but now? Now, he was confused. Cian had made it clear they needed to send Katya on her way, and while Cian had more patience than just about anyone Liam knew, with the possible exception of Finn, he also had the world on his plate at any given time. Liam couldn't continue to put this additional burden on his brother. He had to do something other than slink from safe house to safe house, hoping some magical solution presented itself.

"You are hungry?" asked Katya as she joined him in the kitchen.

"No, but I'm happy to get you something if you are."

He looked at her as she hopped up onto the countertop, swinging her long legs while she watched him. He could tell she had already put on some weight. Eating regular meals and getting enough sleep was helping. Her bruises had faded almost completely, and the dark circles under her eyes were gone as well. Every day that passed, she looked healthier, more relaxed, happier. And Liam had to admit, it made him happy to see her happy. He didn't want to give that up.

"You don't need to always... How do you say? Serve me," she told him. "At home, in Russia, my mother work two jobs. When I was small, an old woman in our hall would feed me. I stay in her apartment. She watch old German soap operas every day, but she at least feed me. When I was old enough for school, I am old enough to feed myself."

"Meanwhile my mother made us three meals a day," he answered her, reaching into the fridge and taking out a loaf of bread and the cheap lunch meat his men had stocked the place with. "Breakfast, lunch, and dinner, seven days a week, our whole lives. And before we moved out, she taught us how to make a few things for ourselves—you've pretty much seen everything I'm able to cook."

He began putting together the boring sandwich, then found some chips and a soda as well, before presenting it all to Katya on a paper plate.

"But this isn't cooking, this is assembly. So have some of what I've assembled. I don't mind serving you."

She laughed softly, and he smiled back at her, and for the first time since he was sixteen years old, Liam MacFarlane wanted to think about what was going to happen more than twenty-four hours into the future.

But what would that future look like? Liam couldn't bring a single image to mind—not one that included him anyway. All he saw when he thought of the word "future" was his brother Connor, standing on a beach somewhere, looking at the ocean with the love of his life, Jess, at his side. He saw Connor in a tux getting married, standing over a crib looking at a baby, getting an award at a restaurant he managed. When Liam thought about a future, he thought about Connor. And that was telling in and of itself.

Why had he never thought more than twenty-four hours ahead? When had he become so entrenched in living life from one act of violence to the next that he'd forgotten to dream, to hope, to plan?

"What did you want?" he asked. "When you decided to come to the US, before you realized what they had planned for you, what did you want?"

Katya's smile dimmed, but her eyes grew dreamy. "I want to be free—free from no money, free from life with my mother, free from fear I turn into her. I did not expect to be rich in America, I want to be alive. In Russia, my mother was like dead, our home was like dead, our world was like dead. The rich are more rich, and we are more poor every day. It is a weight on you, and it makes you dead inside, even when you walk as if you are alive."

With a blinding clarity, Liam suddenly understood exactly what she meant. Because poverty didn't just come from lack of money, it could come from lack of love, lack of security, lack of companionship. And poverty could come from lack of hope. He realized that in the last sixteen years—half his damn life—he too had been dead inside. Since the day his father pointed a gun at his head and told Cian to make a choice, Liam had lived without hope.

Liam's bank account might not be impoverished, but his soul certainly was.

"You are nowhere near dead," he said, involuntarily taking a step toward her. His voice was fierce with conviction as he continued. "Even after everything you've been through, you are full of life—you love your friend, Nadja, you keep fighting to stay alive, you're learning to trust me even after I abandoned you." He stepped closer again and saw her pupils dilate, but somehow he knew it wasn't with fear.

"I know what it feels like to be dead inside. I've lived that way my whole adult life. But when I saw you tied to that chair, something came to life in me. Something that's still growing. It's taking time, but it's there. I feel it, and the life inside you is what gave it to me."

Her lips parted, and Liam knew he was going to do it, knew it was a foregone conclusion. In the back of his mind, he hoped it wouldn't ruin everything, but the rest of his mind and body couldn't be bothered to weigh that risk. He had to show her, show her how alive both of them still were.

So he reached out, cupping her cheek in one big palm, and pressed his lips to hers. A small gasp escaped her, and she was very still for a few moments as he brushed his mouth against her pillowy flesh.

His hand slid around to the back of her head, his fingers burrowing into her long, wavy hair.

"You're bringing me back to life, and I don't know how I can ever thank you for that."

She blinked at him, her big eyes wise and vulnerable at the same time.

"Why I believe you?" she asked softly, turning her cheek into his caress. "I have never known good man, from man who fathered me and left before I was born, to men who paid for me—and you are not good man. You tell me this yourself. So why do I believe you when you say I bring you back to life?"

He chuckled softly, leaning his forehead against hers. "I don't know," he answered, his voice gruff. "I don't deserve your belief, and I sure as hell don't deserve your kisses, but I'm feeling really damn lucky to have them both right now."

She grinned then. "You are strange man, Liam MacFarlane. But for now, you are strange man who makes me feel more alive too."

Liam's heart soared, and he kissed her again, with more intensity, finally breaking after several minutes of tangling tongues. His breath came hot and heavy. "I don't want to push you too fast," he whispered. "You've been through so much."

She gave him a sad smile. "I think we both have. And I think if kisses make us feel more alive, then maybe kisses are okay."

Yes, thought Liam, kisses with Katya made him feel more alive than anything else ever had. And now he had a future to think about—a future of kissing Katya Volkova.

**

Cian looked at the thick Kevlar strapped to Lila's thin frame and knew it wasn't going to work.

"Dammit!" he spat.

"I'm sorry," Danny said. "I double-checked with Liam to make sure this was the smallest we could get. If she were a man, we'd put a suit on her, and it would cover it. But if she's gonna dress like a girl, there's no way to hide this thing."

Finn helped Lila remove the thick vest. "Look, the fact is, if they decide to kill her, it's going to be a headshot."

Cian watched as Lila grew pale. "Jesus, Finn, a little sensitivity, will you?"

"Sorry, Lila." Finn shrugged. "Just telling it like it is."

"And yes, if they're trying to kill her, the vest might not help. But if there's a shootout, it could save her life."

"It's fine," Lila said brusquely. "I never expected I would be going in with any kind of protection. I can't bring Danny." She smiled at the big guard, and Cian watched Danny's face flush in response. He knew Danny had a soft spot for Lila, and it should have pissed him off, but if it meant Danny took better care of her, then Cian couldn't find fault. "I can't bring a weapon. I can't wear armor. It's part of the deal, and I knew that when I asked for the meeting. You have a wire on me. I know you'll come as fast as you possibly can if something goes wrong. It's fine," she finished.

Cian had been in this business long enough to know better than to focus on what he couldn't control. So he focused on what he could. "Tell me again what you're going to say to them," he directed.

He heard Danny sigh. Lila rolled her eyes, and Finn chuckled. But he didn't give a damn. This was Lila. This was life or death.

"I'll explain why Xavier isn't real, I'll tell them the last thing I heard was that Liam and the Russian girl had left town, then I'll tell them you're running scared. That you didn't give Liam permission to take the girl, and you're looking to have a meeting."

"And if they ask you how you have this information?" Finn prompted.

"I'll say that *you* confided in me, that Cian is threatening to close down the sales at Rogue and you're pissed because this project was yours, so you confided in me."

Finn looked at Cian, and Cian could see the sympathy in his brother's eyes. Finn knew how much Cian didn't want to let Lila do this. But Finn was nothing if not rational, so he also knew this was an opportunity they shouldn't pass up.

"She's got it," Finn said softly.

"Yeah, she does."

There was a light knock on the door, then Louis stuck his head in. "It's time to go, boss."

"We'll meet you out back," Finn said, tipping his chin to Danny to indicate they should leave Lila and Cian alone for a moment.

After the other men had left, Cian and Lila stood silently looking at one another. "Are you sure?" His voice was so soft, it was almost a whisper.

She nodded.

"I'll never forgive myself if something happens to you."

She stepped closer to him, wrapping her hand around the back of his neck as she pressed her chest against his. "That's okay. I have enough forgiveness for both of us." She touched his lips briefly with her own, then stepped back and walked out the door.

**

She knew the man she was facing was Sergei even before he told her. He stood an average height, barrel-chested, with sharp blue eyes, and gray hair cut brutally short. He had a scar that ran from the outside edge of one eyebrow down to his cheekbone. But in spite of all that, there was something charismatic about him—cruel but compelling. No way was a man like him not the leader of the group of truly soulless men arrayed in front of her.

The meeting took place in the parking lot of an abandoned coffee warehouse. Cian had been unwilling to budge on an indoor meet, so Lila had suggested the property. It was technically in MacFarlane territory, but close enough to Consuelos's part of Chicago to make the Russians comfortable. She'd driven herself there in her little Nissan Leaf, but of course, Cian, Danny, Finn, and Louis were waiting in an SUV a few blocks away. The listening device Cian had given her was the size of a pencil eraser and hidden in the snap of her denim jacket.

"Well," Sergei said as he circled her appraisingly. "While I appreciate Mr. Rossi's gift, I don't need more product." He stopped and faced her, his expression cold as ice. "I asked to meet with him, not his secretary."

Lila fought the urge to cross her arms. Cian had coached her on body language—how to avoid looking defensive, scared, unsure. The trick, he'd told her, was to appear cool and confident at all times. Easier said than done.

She put her hands in the front pockets of her casual black wool slacks. She'd forgone her usual T-shirt and jeans for something a little more significant, something that said she was a self-confident adult businesswoman. She wondered if she was fooling Sergei even a little bit.

With a small smile, she raised an eyebrow. "I *am* Mr. Rossi," she said slowly. "I have been all along."

Sergei's eyes narrowed. "Not possible. We have seen photos of Xavier Rossi. You think we're so stupid we don't vet our associates?"

Lila began to pace—just a few steps one direction, then the other, back and forth in front of Sergei. He watched her, stone-faced, violence rolling off him like waves on a beach.

"You saw pictures of my former employee, Xavier Rossi. He was an adequate hacker who didn't mind being the face of Rogue. But I own Rogue, I always have, and I'm the one who's communicated with you all these months."

Sergei raised one eyebrow, and his gaze shot to the man at his left, who shrugged lightly to indicate he had no idea what was going on either.

Sergei took a step closer to Lila, and she braced

herself, stopping and facing him head-on.

"You expect me to believe that Xavier Rossi is a real man, but not who I have been communicating with all these months?"

"Yes," Lila answered firmly. She hoped. "Surely you realize that in my world, being a woman is not an advantage. I've used male pseudonyms for years. It gained me respect and kept me safer. And I could have kept on doing it, but you insisted on a face-to-face."

Sergei looked her up and down again, the filth in his mind blatantly obvious in his gaze. "So where has Mr. Rossi gone now?"

"He got greedy. He seemed to forget that he was only a figurehead, so I fired him."

Sergei nodded, but his expression was so stony, she had no idea if he believed her or not. "And you are?"

She swallowed down the bile that rose in her throat. "You can call me Jessamine," she said, using her hacker name.

His eyes narrowed, but he didn't challenge her further. "So tell me this, then, Jessamine. Where is Liam MacFarlane and the item he stole from me?"

Lila's heart raced, and she had to swallow once before she could answer. "The word is he took the woman and left town. I heard his brothers talking about it yesterday, while I was waiting to meet with them about new sales numbers."

"Why would he leave town? He's their head of security, no?"

"Their enforcer. Yes."

Sergei's eyes narrowed. "He's a warrior. He wants war. This is why he took my item. He wanted to start something. None of the information I have on him tells me he would run like a little girl. We had reliable intelligence that said he was in a safe house not far from here only yesterday. We found the house, and it looked as though they had just left."

"Much of that's true, except he didn't count on the fact his older brother wouldn't want the war."

"Continue," Sergei instructed.

Lila shifted her weight from one leg to the other, valiantly trying not to cross her arms in the protective stance Cian had warned her against. "I talked to one of Cian's guards. I told him I was worried about the tension between the Devils and you. That I was afraid it would impact our sales through my website. He told me Liam had taken the woman from you without permission. That Cian had no idea Liam was going to do it, and when he found out, he was livid.

"Cian told Liam he refused to go to war. So Liam took the woman and left town. I can't promise you he won't be back, but he's gone for now."

Sergei stepped closer again, and Lila stiffened. He was within arm's reach now. He could do anything to her he wanted, but to move away would tell him how truly frightened she was. So she lifted her chin, squared her shoulders, and stood her ground.

"And if Cian doesn't want war, how is he expecting this to play out?"

"His guard told me he's running scared, and he wants to meet."

Sergei's expression turned murderous, and Lila flinched. He took the final step into her space, mere inches from her body, his breath hot on her skin, eyes aflame with rage.

"So you told him you were coming to me," he

snarled. "And he instructed you to ask me for a meeting." It wasn't a question.

"No." Lila was proud at how strong her voice sounded when she answered. "I got all this information from his man. Cian has someone guarding me twenty-four seven, and the man has grown...*fond* of me. He only told me to reassure me my business wouldn't be caught in a war between the two of you. I have no idea when Cian might ask for a meeting or where or how. I only know his man told me he wants one, and that he's never seen his boss so scared."

"You tell me he has guards on you around the clock, yet you are here alone?" He put his arms out to the sides in a gesture of disbelief.

Lila shrugged as if it wasn't important. "I told you, he likes me. I said I was going to get some new lingerie and wanted to surprise him. He went for it."

Sergei leaned forward, into her space, his lips beside her ear, his voice low and absolutely deadly. "If I find, little girl, that you have lied to me, I will slit you from here..." His finger touched her between her legs, then he slowly dragged it up her body until he reached the hollow of her throat, "to here," he finished.

He turned, barked an order in Russian to his men, and they all climbed into the car before peeling away out of the parking lot, leaving Lila shaking so hard, she fell to her knees, and heaved up the contents of her stomach.

**

In the front passenger seat of the dark SUV, Cian sat

and white-knuckled the armrest as he listened to Lila vomit. Both he and Danny, who was in the driver's seat, had earpieces and had been privileged to hear Sergei's threats.

"She's okay, boss," Danny assured him. "She held it together when it mattered. She's a warrior."

"Are they gone? Is she okay?" Finn asked from the backseat where he sat with Louis.

Cian heard Lila murmur, "Sorry about that. I'm okay. Getting in the car to leave."

"I'll fucking kill him," Cian ground out, his entire body tense with fury.

"Hey. Update please," Finn reiterated.

Danny's gaze went to the rearview mirror. "She's okay. She's in the car headed our way."

Cian heard Finn's sigh of relief and Louis thanking the Virgin Mother. But it was as if he were hearing it through a long tunnel. Blood rushed to his ears, and hot anger spiked in his blood.

Only a moment later, they saw Lila's tiny car slide by in traffic as they had planned. Danny pulled the SUV out two cars behind her, and they proceeded down the street.

Cian ripped the earpiece out and threw it on the floor, then grabbed his phone from the center console and pressed speed dial five.

"Pull over," he instructed into the phone, his tone harsher than he intended but out of his control all the same.

"Boss?" Danny asked, glancing between the road and Cian.

He couldn't focus on what she was saying, but it wasn't yes. "Don't argue with me, Lila. Pull over now," he barked into the phone again. Cian's head throbbed, and he felt like he wanted to climb out of his own skin.

"Cian," Finn interrupted. "I thought we agreed we wouldn't meet up until later? In case she's being followed."

Danny agreed. "He's right, boss. It's not safe. They could easily have extra men watching her. It's what we would have done."

Cian ignored them all, and spoke into the phone. "Lila from Rogue. Pull. The fuck. Over."

Danny shook his head, and Finn muttered something unintelligible from the backseat. Up ahead, Cian saw Lila's car turn into a small corner gas station. Danny followed, parking the SUV broadside to her Nissan Leaf so it was blocked from the view of the street.

Cian stepped out of the SUV and slammed the door behind him. Lila was out of her car by the time he reached her. He pulled her to one side and closed her car door before pushing her back against it. Holding her shoulders, he looked in her eyes and then quickly scanned her from head to toe and back again.

"Did he touch you?"

Her gaze darted away from his for just a split second, and that was how he knew she was lying when she answered, "No. I'm fine."

"You're lying."

"Does it matter? It's over, I'm fine, and we did what we needed."

He felt Danny hovering behind his right shoulder and saw Lila's gaze go to the burly guard.

"You did good," Danny told her. "You've got balls of steel. I know a lot of men who couldn't have done that."

"Cian. This isn't the time," Finn added. "You have to rein it in. She took a big chance. Let's not undo it by being careless."

Cian looked into Lila's dark eyes and suddenly felt as though all the breath had been taken from him. He struggled to maintain his composure, and as he did, the whole world became crystal clear.

"Put her in our car," he instructed Danny.

"Come on, slugger," Danny said gently. "Our ride is a lot more comfortable anyway."

Cian leaned an arm against Lila's car. He was going to lose it, and he didn't want anyone else to see.

"Take her to Cian's place," Finn instructed. "We'll drive her car back and stash it in the underground."

Cian kept his back to the SUV as he heard Danny start it up and drive away. He leaned into the tiny car, breath tight, heart racing.

Then he felt Finn's hand on his back between his shoulder blades. "Just breathe," Finn instructed, his voice low. "Nice, slow, long breaths."

And as his brother's voice soothed him and his lungs began to let air in again, as he stood in the trashy parking lot of a third-rate gas station and images of Lila split open and bleeding out flashed in front of his eyes, he knew something fundamental had changed. He knew that for the first time in his life, he really did love someone besides his family, and he knew he'd just lost his last leverage in the battle to save his brothers. Because there was no way he could ever sell out Lila.

**

"Do you believe Liam MacFarlane has left town?" Sergei's man asked him as they drove in the car.

"Do you?" Sergei snapped.

The man shrugged, "Maybe, maybe not. If he really wants a war, he would stay. But the girl... She might be enough to make him want something other than war." The man waggled his eyebrows leeringly.

Sergei's lip curled in disgust at the idea a man would put a woman before business. He liked women as much as the next man, but they were good for only one thing, and you certainly didn't need to let them interfere with work in order to have that.

When he arrived back at the brothel, Sergei went straight to his computer specialist. "Have they found another safe house?" he asked.

"They tracked one down, but it was empty. I think it was used even earlier than the other we found."

Sergei's fist clenched in frustration, and he turned to one of his men standing in the doorway. "Get me the girl, Nadja," he demanded.

His man grunted at him. "Of course."

Sergei's gut told him something about all this wasn't right. His gut had kept him alive all these years, so he relied on it heavily. Why had Liam stolen the girl in the first place? And had he really left town now? Sergei doubted it, but he couldn't be certain. Was Cian running scared? Or had he sent the woman pretending to be Xavier to Sergei as a trick? The damn Irish were worse than the Mexicans. Nothing they did was rational, and it was giving Sergei a headache. For now, he would proceed with caution, take each step one at a time, testing the waters. But before he did anything else, he needed to relieve some stress. Luckily, his new favorite, Nadja, was waiting for him.

He strode down the hallway and threw open the door to his personal room at the brothel. The girl was sprawled naked on the bed, her hair a tangled mess, mascara smeared under her eyes like a raccoon.

She looked at him, eyes glazed over, skin pale, a desperate smile snaking across her face. "I'm so glad to see you," she said. "How can I make you happy tonight?"

He unbuckled his belt and pulled it slowly from the belt loops. He saw her eyes widen, and it made him hard.

"You expect me to believe you want to make me happy?" he asked. "I think you just want more heroin."

He saw the need in her eyes at the mention of the word, and his lip curled in disgust. "You get nothing tonight. At least not until you've satisfied me."

Nadja nodded frantically. "Yes, baby, anything you want." She crawled up onto her hands and knees and made her way down the bed, looking at him as her breasts swayed beneath her. That should've aroused him, but her desperation was pathetic. Luckily, he knew how to fix that.

He reached down and grabbed her hair, wrenching her head back. She cried out in pain, and her eyes watered, he pulled hard until she was raised up on her knees, her eyes nearly level with his. He stared at her for a moment. She had been a beautiful girl, but the drugs had ruined her. They always did. But the weak ones needed them; otherwise, none of the customers wanted to be with them. While many men liked their women fearful, few liked them hysterical.

Yes, Nadja was no use like this anymore, it was time to finish her so he could spend the resources on someone more profitable. But she could still serve a purpose once she was gone. She would be the perfect messenger, possibly the one thing to bring Liam MacFarlane out of hiding. He smiled to himself as he listened to her rapid, shallow breaths and looked into her hazy eyes.

"Don't worry, my dear," he murmured. "You're going to make me happy, and it'll be over very quickly." He unzipped his pants and took his cock out, stroking it slowly as he let his other hand wander down her torso, finding one of her breasts and squeezing it so hard, she yelped in pain. Watching her breath pick up pace and her eyes widen in fear made him even harder. He continued to stroke himself while he drew his hand back and slapped her hard across the face, sending her head snapping violently to one side.

When she looked at him again it was with tears in her eyes and a red handprint on her face. She began begging him to stop. "*Ostanovit'!*" He always loved it when she begged that way.

Pushing her down on her back, he put his hand around her trachea and forced himself into her violently.

Then, as Nadja struggled to eke one more sip of oxygen from the last breath she would ever take, Sergei spent his anger in a roar of triumph. After he was finished, he climbed back to his feet and zipped his pants, looking at her limp body askew on top of the bedcovers. Yes, she was still of use, and wouldn't

Liam MacFarlane and his whore get a treat when they were reunited with her?

Chapter Thirteen

By the time Lila was hustled in the door of Cian's penthouse, the adrenaline crash had come and she was shaking like a leaf.

"Here," Danny said gently as he handed her a mug of tea where she sat on the sofa. "I put in lots of sugar, helps with the shock. You'll be okay."

The mug shook so hard in her hand, she nearly spilled the hot liquid all over herself.

"I'm…really…fine," she said, teeth chattering. "I just can't…s-stop sh-shaking."

"You remember that time after I got shot by some of the Vasquez guys over in Jackson Park?" Louis asked from where he stood by the front door.

"Yeah," Danny answered, watching Lila carefully as she sipped the tea. "You were shaking like a dog after a bath."

"Right? It'll go away in a bit," Louis consoled as he stretched his big arms over his head, exposing the guns that resided under one arm and in the waistband of his khakis.

Lila tried to focus on her breathing, taking small sips of the sweet liquid as she counted inhalations and exhalations. She realized she'd vomited in the parking lot and never had a chance to clean up. God. She probably reeked. She looked down, hoping she wouldn't find puke all over her button-down blouse.

The door to the penthouse burst open, and Cian strode in, Finn right behind him, neither of them looking particularly happy.

Cian came straight to her and dropped to his knees, his brow furrowed in worry. For a long moment, they simply locked gazes, saying a million things all at once, none of them out loud.

"I want to talk to Lila alone," Cian directed, his voice husky. Lila didn't even look away as Danny, Finn, and Louis filed out of the room.

When they were gone, Cian took her hands in his and kissed them on the knuckles. "Never again," he told her. "You can't ever do something like that again."

She swallowed uncomfortably, her throat tight with all of it—the fear, the disgust, the tenderness.

"But I did it," she said, trying...and failing...to smile.

Cian shook his head, releasing her hands and standing as he gazed down at her. "You did it, and you may have gotten a reprieve for Rogue, but now Sergei knows what you look like. It wasn't worth it, Lila. Why can't you see that?"

She dropped her gaze, not wanting him to see that he might be right. When Sergei had touched her, when he'd leaned in and whispered that in her ear, she'd known she'd gone too far. She had never been so frightened in her life. Never felt less in control, less able, less worthwhile. Cian had been right, Sergei wasn't just a criminal. He was something else. Something darker, more insidious. Something evil.

Setting the mug down on the coffee table in front of her, Lila breathed.

"We're hitting their utilities tonight," she said, deciding that a change of subject was in order.

Cian nodded, not looking at her as he leaned one elbow against the mantel of the fireplace. "Good."

"How are Liam and Katya?"

"Fine. For now."

She tried one last time. "If I get back to work on that overseas account, I think I can crack it in the next few hours. I was very close earlier this morning."

This time, he didn't respond at all.

She finally stood, crossing the room to stand alongside him. "I'm sorry."

He didn't look at her.

"Maybe I shouldn't have done it… I don't know anymore, Cian. I don't know how you do this. How you keep track of the pieces and make these life-and-death decisions all the time. I don't know what your long game is, but I know you well enough to assume you have one. How you're balancing that with the shorter term and the crises that seem to pop up minute by minute, I'll never understand."

He glanced down at her, and she took that as a sign to press harder, so she scooted around to face him.

"I don't know how you do this," she repeated before she placed her hand over his heart. "I think I know *why* you do it. But I don't know *how*."

His gaze drifted to her face, her lips, her throat,

then to her hand where it touched him.

"I'm not sure I can keep doing it much longer," he murmured. "Not when I see Liam's apartment's been blown to bits with him in it. Not when I hear a man like Sergei threaten to cut you open while I'm sitting blocks away, completely helpless."

"I'm sorry. You were right, I didn't understand. He's something more than just a gangster. He's…"

"I think the word you're looking for is insane." Cian placed his hand over hers. "The Bratva are known for it. They're not businessmen like a lot of the guys I deal with. They're known for the lengths they'll go to in order to get revenge or prove a point. They're insane, plain and simple."

Lila took a deep breath, and before she could stop herself, she blurted it out, that thing deep inside that had been gnawing at her since the first night she'd slept in Cian's arms. The thing that had brought her to this place, this point, this precipice.

"I don't want to leave." Her face flushed with heat.

He smiled tenderly at her, and it nearly broke her in pieces.

"And I don't want you to leave." Then he paused, and she knew what came next. "But you have to."

He was right. But it hurt.

"I know I can't make you, and I can't tell you when, but you have to promise me that you will."

She swallowed, her throat dry with anxiety. "Okay. I promise."

He pulled her to him in a close embrace, leaning his lips next to her ear. She couldn't help but think how entirely different it felt from Sergei's lips in the same position. A shudder ran through her from head to toe.

"Listen carefully," he whispered into her hair. "There is a car parked in the covered lot at Adams and Racine, slot seventeen, for the date we first met. Inside the glove box is a passport with your photo, cash, and a number to call for a chartered plane to Nauru. Once that number is called, the plane will be waiting by the time you arrive at the airstrip, and things will be set in motion, including a customs agent who will meet you when you land and expedite your paperwork."

She started to pull away from him to look at his face, but he held her tight, talking faster, his voice still in a whisper.

"There is a house there for you, with a staff— housekeeper, guards, grounds people. And in the house, there are the numbers for offshore accounts that will last you the rest of your life. You can take your mother with you--"

Now she did pull away. "Cian, no…"

He gazed at her, and that was when she realized. That was when she knew that the deep ache she'd been carrying around since the day they first met was shared, and that it wasn't just attraction or lust or friendship, it was love. She'd fallen in love with Cian MacFarlane, just as he'd fallen in love with her.

"Yes," he said emphatically. "Yes. I told you I'd take care of you, and I meant it."

"I can take care of myself—"

"I know that," he interrupted. "I know you could get your own IDs and stash your own money—I assume you have, in fact. You're far more capable of disappearing than I am. But I wanted to do this. I needed to. I have to know you'll be okay. When all this is over—when Liam and Finn are out too—I want to be able to picture you in that house, the one I gave you, being protected by the people I'm paying for. Safe. And happy. I really want you to be happy, Lila."

"What if I can't be happy without you?" she asked in a small voice, her chest split open with the pain of it all.

He held her cheeks in his palms and kissed her on the forehead. "You can. I promise you can."

"So *this* is your long game? You get Liam and Finn and me out like you did Connor, and then you what? Take the fall? Let yourself get killed? If you can get us out, why can't you save yourself?"

"That's not how this particular scenario works." His gaze left hers as he looked over her head out the windows. "The friends that I deal with?"

She nodded, knowing he meant the FBI.

"I'm arranging for them to let my brothers go. One at a time. My friends don't know that, but…" He shrugged.

"No!" she cried.

"Shh, shh," he warned, tipping his chin back toward the other side of the penthouse where Finn, Louis, and Danny had gone and the soft murmur of a television played.

"You can't," she whisper-yelled, terror lodging deep in her gut. "You can't make yourself the trade-off."

"I can, and I have. There's no way out of this for me." Then he kissed her softly on the lips. "But there is for you, and that's what matters. You've promised me now, and I know you won't go back on that. Tell me where the car is parked."

She dutifully repeated the information back to him, and he grinned, seemingly satisfied.

"Good. Now, I want you to stay here until you go. I don't care how many men I keep on that place of yours, it has ground floor access and all those windows, it's impossible to really secure it."

She sighed, too drained and overwrought to argue anything more. "Okay.

"I'll have the guys bring all your stuff over—your computers, clothes, what else?"

"Everything in the top left drawer of the bathroom."

He grinned and gave her a smacking kiss on the lips. "We'll play house, Lila from Rogue. Until you go, we'll play house. And it will give me something to remember. It's the best gift I could ask for."

Lila managed to smile back, while deep inside, something cracked and then shattered. She might have gone her whole life and never encountered Cian MacFarlane, and that was tragic yet wishful thinking all at the same time.

Because once upon a time, Lila Rodriguez had thought her father was the man to break her, but now she realized it was Cian who would do it instead.

**

The power at the brothel went out at ten p.m., right at the start of their highest traffic of the day. Sergei followed one of his men down the hallway to the control box, their way lit only by the flashlight on a cell phone.

"All these breakers are on," Alexei told him.

"The streetlights are still on outside," another man said, entering the room.

"*Yebat',*" Sergei swore. The MacFarlanes. "Find Liam MacFarlane," he growled.

"We don't even know if he's still in town," Alexei answered.

"*Find him!*" Sergei roared before planting his fist deep in the other man's gut. As Alexei collapsed to the floor, clutching his midsection, Sergei kicked him hard in the face before slamming out of the room.

**

Liam was fully dressed, curled around Katya's sleeping body. They'd kissed for hours, but only kissed, because he figured, with everything she'd been through, anything else had to be up to her. As he'd tamped down the urge to tear her clothes off and bang her on the kitchen counter, he'd reminded himself of his purpose—to give her back her choices.

So he'd kissed her, and kissed her and kissed her, like some teenager making out in front of the TV. And she'd let him. And then they'd fallen asleep. Or she had.

Something in Liam's gut wasn't right, and he always trusted his gut.

He almost dismissed the first whistle, but when it was followed by a second and then a muffled thump, he reached for his gun on the coffee table next to him. As he began to sit up, Katya complained, still asleep, murmuring something in Russian. He shook her as gently as he could, leaning down and whispering in her ear.

"You have to wake up. Don't make a sound."

In the light that filtered in from outside, he could see her eyes pop open, wide with fear. He held a finger to his lips, and she nodded, silently. They both sat up, and Liam swung his feet to the floor, wincing a touch as his ribs protested. He was healing well, but Katya's weight against his chest had aggravated the bruises.

She sat, frozen, waiting for him to tell her what to do. He listened, his internal radar telling him something bad was coming. He heard another subtle thump and saw Katya flinch. Yeah, it wasn't him being paranoid; she could feel it too.

Without pausing for a moment, he grabbed her by the wrist and bolted off the sofa, tugging her through the door to the bathroom just as the first bullets sprayed in through the back windows of the living room.

The house was a tiny bungalow—living room, kitchen, bathroom, and one bedroom. The bathroom was dominated by an old claw-foot tub, and the only window was the small one over it. Liam closed the door, putting Katya in front of him with his back to the wood that would last about ten seconds once they entered the house and continued shooting.

"Get down in the tub," he instructed as he stepped onto the edge of it and leaned over to unlatch the window.

She huddled, arms tucked around her knees.

"Get your head down too," he instructed, sounding harsher than he intended. She complied immediately.

The rusty latch resisted, then gave way suddenly, making a screech. Liam took a deep breath and paused, listening to the sounds of renewed shots rocketing through the living room. He couldn't help but chuckle. They were scared of him, ripping up the place with round after round before they dared to kick in the door and face whatever might be inside.

Pussies.

He slowly pushed the little window open, keeping his head below the frame in case someone outside noticed and shot. But then he heard a whisper.

"Liam! Liam!"

He stood taller and peeked over the edge of the sill to find Jimmy staring back at him from the alley below the window.

Thank God, the Russians hadn't killed both of his men.

"Hey," he said quietly.

"I have the car around the corner. I was doing a walk-around when they hit. Must have thought there was only the one of us up front."

Liam nodded as he heard the front door splinter and voices shouting in Russian.

"Take Katya. I'll never fit through this window. Don't wait. I'll catch up," he instructed. Jimmy didn't look happy, but he nodded.

Liam reached down and pulled Katya to standing. "Go with Jimmy. He'll take care of you."

"But what about—"

"Just do what I say." He didn't give her a chance to respond to that, just grabbed her around the hips and boosted her headfirst through the window. Jimmy grabbed her arms and pulled her the rest of the way out. Liam heard their footsteps running down the alley and saw Katya looking behind her, trying to watch him as Jimmy pulled her away.

Liam pulled one gun out of his waistband and another from an ankle holster. He said a quick Hail Mary, then carefully cracked the bathroom door open. He heard the men in the kitchen, and heavy boots heading toward the back of the house where the bathroom and bedroom were located. Any moment, he was going to be trapped like a rat in a cage.

With lightning speed, he burst out of the bathroom, landing in the archway between the living room and back hallway. He noted one man with his back turned in the doorway to the kitchen, and another to his left, heading right for him. He fired with both guns, hitting the guy in the kitchen square in the back and winging the other guy in the shoulder, causing him to drop his gun.

Shouting came from the kitchen, and Liam knew there was at least one more man in the house. He didn't waste time to find out, but instead darted into the bedroom, picked up the nightstand, and tossed it through the plate-glass window, leaping through the sharp-edged opening seconds before the bedroom door slammed open and bullets flew. He ran alongside the house wall until he reached the corner, then he took off running, leaping over fences, and landscaping, darting between yards, sticking to private properties rather than the street where he would be so much more visible.

An hour later, after hiding five separate times from the Russians cruising the area looking for him, he bought a burner at a convenience store and stood outside the concrete-block building along the darkened side, away from the parking lot and any lights.

He punched in Cian's number, and his

overprotective older brother answered on the first ring.

"Where are you?"

"How did you know it was me?" Liam asked, amused.

"Just tell me where the hell you are so we can come pick you up," Cian snarled in response.

"Is Katya okay?"

"Yes, she's fine. We're all here at my place baking cookies while we wait to find out if you're *alive*."

Scratching his head, he glanced up at the sky. Not a single star shone in the light-polluted sky, and for a moment, he wondered what the sky was like in Russia where she'd come from. Were there stars for her to wish on? Jewels in the night sky to decorate her drab existence? Somehow, he doubted it. Somehow, he felt like Katya's world had always been as lacking in natural light as his.

"I'm okay, and I'm at a Quik Stop on Fourth near Amstead."

"We'll be there in ten minutes," Cian said, then he disconnected.

Liam rounded the back corner of the building and slumped against the rough wall, looking at the weed-choked patch of gravel that housed the dumpster and a few dozen broken bottles. Kissing Katya already seemed like a lifetime ago. He couldn't admit it to anyone else, but he had to admit it to himself—he was tired. And while a few days ago this had seemed like more of what his life usually was, right now, it felt an awful lot like something he'd hoped to never experience again—prison.

Liam's time in prison was something he'd never spoken about with anyone. Yes, Cian had asked a few questions afterward, but Liam could tell it pained him to hear it, so it became a topic they all avoided. He'd known going in that it would be the toughest thing he'd ever faced, and by that point, he'd faced some pretty tough stuff. But while he'd prepared his body for every bit of it, his spirit had been another challenge.

Because it was your spirit that they tried to break in prison—the part of you that believed in yourself, the part of you that had autonomy of thought and emotion and belief. The part of you that was the master of your free will. Prison took that from you, through the degradation and humiliation, through the constant threat of violence, through the physical limitations. Prison wasn't really about protecting others or rehabilitation or even retribution. Prison was about breaking you, plain and simple.

There was no recipe for mending you once you'd been broken either, no method for piecing a man back together. There was only the breaking of spirit, the crushing of free will, the destruction of choice. And when prison was done with you, it spit you back out into a world you'd never survive. Because prison had made sure you couldn't.

It had taken everything Liam had to keep from breaking those few months he'd been inside. And for the first time in his life, he'd had to be grateful to his father. Robbie had prepared him about as well as someone could be. He'd taught Liam never to trust, never to let down his guard, never to give in. But while Liam had sat in that cell day after day, losing his mind with worry over Cian and Connor and Finn, struggling to avoid the worst that prison could offer, forced to be the worst, hardest version of himself every hour of every day, he'd begun to think about what it meant that his father was the one who had prepared him for it.

What kind of a world did Liam come from where his own father had given him the lesson that enabled him to survive hell? It was a thought that circled his head over and over during those months. But then he'd been released, and he'd been so relieved, so happy to be back in the real world, so determined not to ever get caught again, he'd put it out of his mind. Much the way he'd put what Robbie had done all those years ago out of his mind.

But now he'd been trapped in safe houses, watching Katya as she struggled to recover from her own prison experience, and it had all come flooding back. The way it felt to have to fight that spirit-breaking pressure day after day. The thoughts he'd had when he sat in his cell for hours on end, trapped and vulnerable. The moment he'd realized his father had done him a favor by holding a gun to his head.

And now, as he hid, yet again, from more men who wanted to break him—permanently—he knew exactly what Katya meant when she said she only wanted to be free.

And in a moment of insight, he also knew why he was drawn to Katya in a way he'd never been to another woman. She'd faced the same thing he had—she'd faced a prison that tried to break her spirit, and she'd fought back. The moment she'd sat in that room, beaten and confined, and turned him away because she refused to leave her friend, he'd known. Here was a woman who would not let them break her.

And that was the moment his spirit recognized

hers. The moment he couldn't forget, couldn't let disappear. He hadn't gone back out of guilt, not really. He'd gone back because he knew her. He knew her so deeply and profoundly that he'd recognize her anywhere, anytime. She could wear a million different skins, and still he would know her.

"Damn," he muttered, casting his gaze to the starless sky.

He knew Katya Volkova's soul. And that changed everything.

Chapter Fourteen

It was seven a.m. when Sergei realized his personal bank accounts had been emptied. It was seven oh six when he ripped the scrawny nerd who handled tech for him out of one of the beds at the whorehouse, leaving the brunette who'd been sleeping next to him screaming in terror.

He marched the naked, shivering man to the office where the computers were, gun at his head. When he had the useless waste of employee space seated in front of the large monitor at the desk, he tapped the barrel of the gun on the screen.

"Five million dollars," he snarled. "It is missing. From the bank accounts you swore to me were impenetrable. Five. Million. American. Dollars." His voice rose with every word, and the rage took over as he clocked the nerd on the cheekbone with the butt of his gun. The man yelped in pain as his cheek split open.

"I want that money back in my accounts in

twelve hours," Sergei commanded. "And if it's not..." He leaned down and put his face in front of the nerd's. He could smell the man's fear—sweat, blood, piss. "I will slice your balls off before I kill you."

The man didn't even answer, simply began typing frantically on the keyboard. Three hours later, five million dollars disappeared from a small bank on the island of Kiribati. It was the entire holdings of the island's main nonprofit foundation, which had to shut down the next day. But Sergei hadn't specified *which* five million dollars he wanted, only that the amount be in his bank before the deadline. And the fact was, the tech nerd had no idea where the original money had gone. It had vanished into thin air.

**

There was a time when five million dollars would have made Robbie ecstatic. But this wasn't that time. He knew what it was—an effort on Cian's part to placate him, silence him, neuter him.

"I don't need money," he answered as Cian sat watching him.

"Well, be that as it may, you now have five million more than you did when you woke up."

Robbie snorted. "Until they figure out how to do the same thing to us, and back and forth it goes. There's only one way to ensure they can't come after us more—it's called killing them."

Cian tensed, that look of tight anger crossing his face. Robbie wanted to wipe it the hell off.

"No," Cian said flatly. "I've explained we don't have the resources—the soldiers—to do that. I'm not going to bring the New York Bratva down on us. This is their number two guy. He'll have plenty of support from his higher-ups in Brooklyn."

"And if I say do it anyway?" Robbie stared down the boy he'd once upon a time thought could replace him.

Cian stared back. "Then you'll have to do it on your own. You know most of the men will follow me. You want to hustle up some of the old ones who would follow you on a suicide mission, you go ahead, but don't think I'll back you, and don't think I won't sever our relationship when the Russians strike back. I'll disavow you like head lice."

"You wouldn't dare." Robbie stood from his chair.

Cian stepped closer, and Robbie could see the hate in his eyes. But the feeling was mutual. This weak, posturing excuse for an heir didn't have the steel to follow through. He was empty threats and false promises.

"Try me." Cian's gaze was like ice in an arctic front off Lake Michigan.

Robbie took a deep breath and knew it was time to reassess. He couldn't crush Cian with force, Angela would never forgive him. No, he had to do it in a way she'd never find out about. He needed time to plan it, time to think. His heart tightened like it was in a vise, the sign he'd let his emotions get the better of him.

"Fine." He turned away so Cian couldn't see him grimace in pain. "You do what you're going to do, but I want a full report every single day. And I want the Russian woman gone in the next twenty-four hours." He stood facing the window, not even seeing the flowers Angela had planted outside. His focus was entirely on the breathing and self-control he needed to keep his heart from crushing itself.

"I'll have someone stop by to update you each morning," Cian answered coldly.

Robbie heard his son's footsteps fade away down the hall, and finally collapsed in his chair, panting with exertion. His head throbbed, and he wheezed out a breath as he clutched at his chest.

"Robert?" Angela's voice came from the doorway.

"I'm okay," he ground out. "Just need a minute."

"Get the oxygen," he heard Angela order one of the staff. "And the wheelchair!"

Robbie spent the remainder of his day in bed with his beautiful wife fussing over him. It gave him lots of time to plan how he was going to bring Cian to heel once and for all. He couldn't kill the kid, so he had to make him obey, and it was pretty obvious that while Cian was weak on enemies, he was endlessly defiant with his father.

As Robbie calculated how to take away the things Cian valued most in life, he decided being a parent really was the hardest job in the world.

**

"She did it?" Liam asked as he stood in the tiny back alley of the seedy apartment building he and Katya had just arrived at after a night at Cian's penthouse.

Cian nodded. "She did. Five million disappeared from Sergei's accounts earlier this morning."

Liam smiled. "Damn. I bet that didn't sit well."

"Guarantee it."

Liam leaned one shoulder against the brick wall.

"But you're not all that pleased…"

"No, it's great, but they'll hit back, whether it's with guns or tech." He paused, and Liam saw a storm brewing in his brother's face.

"What's going on?" he asked, ready to fight whatever it was. No one messed with Cian, it was Liam's one defining rule in life. Anyone who tried answered to him, his men, and his guns. Period.

Cian looked uncomfortable as he ran a hand along the back of his neck, always his tell when he didn't want to say something.

"Just spit it out. Things can't get much worse."

"Pop is insisting Katya go."

Liam's heart beat hard once, and he swallowed. "We don't listen to Pop all that well these days, from what I can tell."

"True." Cian looked up into Liam's eyes. Ah, so that was it.

"But you think he's right," Liam finished.

Cian's sigh was long and slow. "I do. She's serving no purpose at this point, and she'd be safer a long way from here. She makes you vulnerable, and I'd like to have you back in the game rather than hiding out. You're a lot easier to protect alone than you are with her."

Liam pushed off the wall and turned to face the alleyway. It was narrow, full of leftover trash and half-opened dumpsters. Broken glass and needles littered the ground, and he couldn't help but think of how many places like this he'd stood in over the last few days. It was starting to become a habit.

His head hurt, and his heart hurt, but his brother was right—his brother was always right. It was a fundamental part of Liam's belief system. Cian was older, wiser, and really fucking brave. He was also always right.

"Yeah, okay. How fast can we get her documents and a ticket out of here?"

"Already done. I just need to know where the plane's going."

Yeah, that was Cian too. Always thinking a step ahead. Liam had a plan for how to exit the apartment they were in if it was shot up like the last place. He hadn't thought beyond that.

"Okay, I'll ask her today."

Cian's hand landed heavily on Liam's shoulder. "You did a good thing, rescuing her. I'm proud of you."

He nodded, about to say the words *thank you*, even though his insides were knotted up like something a Boy Scout had tied, when a high-pitched scream ripped through the air above their heads.

"That was Katya," he shouted even as his feet were already moving. He wrenched open the metal door to the building, Cian hot on his heels. They pounded up the backstairs to the landing on the third floor, where one door stood ahead of them and another was thrown open on the opposite end of the landing.

Jimmy stood holding a sobbing Katya as Liam flew around the stair railing, blood boiling, gun drawn.

"What is it?" he demanded, about to shove past Jimmy and Katya to slay whatever lay in the apartment. He felt Cian hovering at his shoulder, ready to take charge.

"It's all clear inside," Jimmy said as Katya's sobs tore a hole in Liam's heart. "But the Russians had already found this place before we got here, I guess." He tipped his head toward the interior of the apartment. "Bathroom."

Liam strode inside, Cian at his back, and when he reached the tiny bathroom, his knotted insides threatened to lurch out of his mouth. He'd seen a lot of gruesome things in his life, but he'd never seen something so intensely personal in its grotesqueness.

In the bathtub lay a body—female, young, dark hair. Her throat was circled in dark, livid bruises, her arms positioned so the track marks were clear. One leg was draped over the edge of the tub so her genitals were exposed. They were swollen, red and raw, and Liam winced when he looked.

But worse than all that, worse than the clouded vacant look in the eyes that were wide open, worse than the way one of her ankles appeared to be broken, the foot at an odd angle to the leg, worse than the matted hair and smeared makeup that covered her once-beautiful face, was what had been done to her torso.

Her entire front was sliced from crotch to throat. Then a layer of skin had been peeled back on both sides of the slit, with a note safety-pinned to the edges of the flaps on both sides.

I enjoyed every moment with her, the first line read.

And you're next, the second continued.

"Holy shit," Cian gasped as he looked over Liam's shoulder. Liam took a short, sharp breath through his teeth before closing his eyes. But the visual was there still, burned onto his retinas.

"It's Nadja," he said softly.

"Who?"

"Her friend. I've never seen her, but it has to be

Katya's best friend, Nadja."

"The one she didn't want to leave behind?" Cian asked.

"Yeah. This is my fault," Liam murmured, gaze fixed on the needle marks up and down her smooth, pale arms. "All my fault."

"Bullshit," Cian responded vehemently. "This is that sick fuck Sergei's fault, and don't you dare say otherwise.

"I'll get Finn and the guys over to do cleanup, tell Jimmy to take the bags to my car downstairs, and warn him to watch for eyes. They knew we were coming here. They've tapped into our phones somehow is my guess."

Liam nodded woodenly. He wasn't sure of everything Cian had just said, but he knew he needed to get Katya. Get her and take her away from this. Away from the Russians, away from the war, away from the world he lived in. Never once in his life had Liam considered something other than what he'd been handed. But right then, he decided what he'd been handed wasn't good enough for Katya. She deserved better. She deserved that freedom she talked about, and damn if he didn't want to be the one to give it to her.

Chapter Fifteen

After they'd relocated yet again and Katya had cried herself to sleep, Liam sat, gun in hand, watching her as his mind worked overtime to stop replaying the scene from the dingy apartment bathroom. Instead, he tried to think beyond how he was going to make it through tonight. He tried to think about something more than where the exits were, what the battle plan should be, and how he'd live to see another day.

Liam thought about the future. He wanted Katya to have one, but when he pictured it, he pictured himself there too. Someplace safe, where they could both take a breath. Someplace they could walk the streets, hand in hand, and just....be. A life where they didn't need guards outside the door and guns in every drawer.

But that future wasn't in Chicago. It wasn't with his brothers, and it didn't include protecting Cian, which was Liam's life's work.

And then he thought of Connor. His baby

brother, the hothead of the family, and the only one who'd ever dared to fall in love. Somewhere, Liam wasn't sure where, Connor was sleeping right now, in a bed with his girlfriend, Jess, after having put in a night's work managing a bar. Weeks ago, it had sounded dull as hell. Tonight? It sounded like possibility, like hope, like freedom.

He pulled a burner phone out of his back jeans pocket along with a scrap of paper from his wallet. It wasn't his turn, and Connor wouldn't know the number, so he might not answer, but Liam needed to talk to him. He had to know something.

The line connected, but there was no voice on the other end. *Good job, kid,* Liam thought with pride. He'd taught Connor carefully from the time he was a little boy—trust no one, never let your guard down.

"It's me," Liam said softly.

"Hey, I thought it was Finn's turn. What's happened?" Connor asked, groggy but anxious.

"Everything's fine…well, not necessarily fine, but no one's in the hospital or the morgue or jail."

Connor released a breath. "Good. Good. Okay, so what's up?"

Liam looked at the woman sleeping across the room, and his heart did that thing it always did now when he saw her. Because it knew her and her beautiful warrior soul.

"I have to ask you, now that you're there and settled in and living the day-to-day. Was it worth it?"

There was silence on the other end of the line as Liam waited anxiously for an answer. He didn't realize until it came how much he'd wanted to hear it.

"I miss the hell out of you guys," Connor answered. "I don't want you to think that I don't. I think about you every day. Things I'd tell you, stuff I wish I could do with you."

He chuckled softly, and in that moment, the touch of dark all around him, Liam could physically feel his brother's presence.

"There's this gym here. I've been going to work out a couple of times a week. It's fancier than Sean's place, but still solid. There's a guy I've been sparring with, and he does that thing you were always on me not to, when he lets his left drop before he throws the right?"

Liam listened silently. It had taken him a year or more to break Connor of that habit. He'd finally just had to punch the kid in the face to make him realize how open he was leaving himself. Thank God he hadn't broken his handsome little brother's nose. Their mom would never have forgiven him.

"So every time I spar with this guy, I think about how much I wish it was you there instead. How much I'd love to have you there nagging at me about keeping that hand up."

"But you don't need me there bitching at you anymore, because you already learned," Liam told him.

"It's true. I don't." They were both silent for moment. "But what I'm saying is, I miss you guys even though I don't need you anymore the same way—which isn't what you asked me, is it? Was it worth it? Yes. Even as much as I miss you, it was worth it. And it's not just Jess, man. It's all of it. You know that feeling you have when you wake up in the morning? The way you feel totally relaxed like you could lie there in bed forever and be perfectly happy?"

Liam snorted. "Uh, no. Not since I was a kid anyway."

"Exactly," Connor replied. "I hadn't felt that way since I was a teenager either. It leaves with the life—with the business. But now? Now I wake up, and not only is my girl here with me, but I can breathe. I guess that's how I'd describe it best—I wake up in the morning, and I can breathe."

Liam watched Katya shift in her sleep, making small whimpering noises as she did. She was still reliving it all, throughout the night, throughout the day. When was the last time *she* woke up and could breathe? Really breathe?

"I'm glad," he told Connor. "I'm glad you did it. And I'm sorry I doubted you. You deserve this."

"We all deserve it," Connor answered.

As Liam disconnected the call, he wondered if maybe Connor was right.

✳✳

"How is she doing?" Cian asked when Liam arrived at his condo the next morning before dawn.

"She's really fucking sad," Liam answered, looking pretty worn himself.

"It's no wonder. Even after all these years in this business, that was hard to see. I can't imagine what it was like for a civilian."

Cian walked to the kitchen, and Liam followed. It was still early, so he offered his brother coffee instead of the beer he secretly wanted.

"You looked like you haven't slept." He handed Liam a steaming mug of dark roast.

"I haven't. They've obviously hunted down our

safe houses. I have no idea when they're going to hit next or how. Jimmy and two of the other guys rotated all night so they could each get a couple of hours' sleep, but I couldn't relax enough to do that. I have her out in the car in the garage downstairs, with three guys on her. I don't think we can stay anywhere more than a few hours."

"That's exactly what they want." Cian's brow furrowed in concern at how defeated Liam sounded. "To get you off-kilter, make you anxious, paranoid. But Lila has some more things coming at them today. It might take their attention off you for a bit."

"It won't matter," Liam murmured.

Cian watched his brother. Something was different about him. This wasn't just exhaustion. At least not of the typical variety. This was something more.

"What's going on?" He set down his own cup of coffee.

Liam rolled his shoulders and looked uncomfortable.

"Hey." Cian's voice was sharp. "What is it?"

Liam cleared his throat, then looked Cian in the eye. "When I was locked up, I used to spend so much time worrying about you guys. You especially. I can't stand it when I don't know what you're doing and what guys are watching you. I only let you walk around town because I personally trained these men. They're an extension of me, and they know your safety is the one thing I will never compromise on."

Cian's chest ached suddenly. "I know. And you've kept me safe all these years. You're the best there is, and I'm grateful."

Liam looked away. "But there was something

else I thought about when I was locked up—I used to think how strange it was that Pop is the one who made me able to survive that. He made me prison-worthy, you know?"

Cian's damn heart nearly broke then, and he reached out and put a hand on Liam's shoulder, giving it a quick squeeze. "You're a survivor, and you're the strongest person I know. Pop gets no credit for that. He tried to take away who you were and replace it with fear. He failed. We won. Never forget that."

"But did we? Did we win when we live like this?" He waved his arm around as if the air in the kitchen showed a picture of some sort. "I finally realized last night that I'm fucking homeless. Everything I had—which wasn't much, mind you—was in that apartment. It's been blown the fuck up. I spend my entire life trying to keep from getting killed. It's like I never got out."

"Of jail?"

"Exactly. Because this is just another kind of prison, Cian. And I'm not sure I'm strong enough to survive it forever. Eventually, prison breaks everyone, and I think it's about to break me."

He'd never seen Liam lose his cool like this before. This was the family brute. Their enforcer. Liam had killed men, tortured them, he'd trained every guard they had, and put the fear of God in most of their distributors. Liam didn't get scared, he didn't complain, and he didn't break.

"What are you saying?"

"I'm saying I think I want out."

The room was silent for a long moment, nothing but the hum of the refrigerator and the clicking of the ice maker.

Cian swallowed. He'd worked for nothing more than to keep his brothers safe since he was eighteen. But he'd never thought Liam would want to leave him. Connor and Finn, sure. They weren't made for this life, and Cian had always expected to send them away somehow. But Liam? No, he'd thought Liam would go through witness protection. That the only way he'd get Liam out was if Liam had no other options. He never in a million years thought he'd hear Liam *ask* to leave.

"Out..."

"Of Chicago. Of all of it."

He released a long slow breath. Damn.

"You want to pull a Connor?"

Liam snorted. "With the Russians after me? You think I could just wander off someplace and get a job managing a bar? Get married, have a couple of kids?"

Cian shook his head sadly. "No, I don't. The only way you could get out of all this is if people think you're dead."

Their gazes met, and that was when Cian knew what Liam intended. "And you've already thought of that."

Liam continued to stare at him.

"You want to take Katya and go. Fake your deaths and disappear."

"It's the only way," Liam said sadly. "I did this to myself, but in a way, I almost wonder if I did it *because* I knew there'd be only one way out. Although I don't know that I counted on...her."

Ah. *Now we get to the real issue,* thought Cian.

"So, you and Katya..."

Liam ran a hand across his hair, and for one rare

and pure moment, he looked like a little boy. Not the hard man Robbie had made him, but the kid Cian had grown up with. The one who had come home, crawled into bed with Cian, and cried after their father held a gun to his head, before he'd woken the next morning a different person.

"She's wrecked. So we haven't…but there's something there. She's like me. We understand each other. And I want to help her. I want to give her something. I asked her what she wants most in life, and she said, 'Freedom.' If I can get that for her, then that's what I want to do."

"And you couldn't just send her away for that?" Cian almost wished his brother would do that very thing.

"She needs help, man. Protection, ways to stay off the radar…"

"And you don't want anyone else to do that for her, do you?"

He shrugged.

Cian tried to calm his breathing. This felt so very different than it had with Connor. He'd been relieved as hell to get his baby brother away from all of it. But Liam? Liam was his partner, his backup, the only other person on the planet who knew what had happened to them that night with Robbie. Yes, he'd told himself this was what he wanted, but now it was here? The idea of never seeing Liam again, of letting him walk away, was terrifying.

"You're serious? You barely know her. What if you end up hating her? What if she leaves you? What if she's some sort of total nut job who stabs you in your sleep?"

Liam raised an eyebrow and just stared at Cian.

Yeah, okay, that last one wasn't likely, but the rest of it was probably more than likely.

"Connor had dated Jess for five years. We always knew they'd end up together. He also wasn't you. He'd always done what we do because he'd never been given the option. You—"

Liam stiffened. "I what? *Enjoy* it? I'm really *good* at it? I'm too *stupid* to do anything else?"

Cian stared. Where the hell had that come from? His gut went sour. "No, of course not. I didn't mean…"

"I know you didn't. But it's what people think, and in some ways, they're right. I've never minded who I am or what I do. Until I got locked up. And that was different." His voice lowered, husky with emotion. "It was rougher than I could have imagined, and if I'm being honest, it took a lot out of me." He faced Cian then, and Cian saw it all, laid bare in his eyes, in the way he held his body, in the tone of his voice. "Running from the Bratva, it feels like that again. I don't want to do it anymore. I don't want Katya to have to do it. I want to breathe."

And so Cian wrapped a piece of steel around his heart, and he said the words he wouldn't have dreamed he'd ever say, the ones that took a piece of him he'd never get back. Liam was his best friend, his shield, his history, and with one word, Cian let him go.

"Okay."

"I'll worry about you—"

"It's okay," Cian repeated as much for himself as for Liam.

"We're going to have to lie to Mom."

"I know."

"She'll be heartbroken."

"Eh, it's you. She might not be that upset," Cian said, shoving Liam in the chest. His brother was on him in an instant, punching Cian in the midsection, not hard enough to do any damage, but hard enough Cian felt the air whoosh out of him.

Liam danced away across the kitchen, fists raised above his head. "Yes! Yes! Speed and agility win again."

Cian stood, coughing as he regained his breath. He pointed a finger at Liam in warning. "You're going to pay for that."

Smiling, Liam answered, "I'll be long gone, brother. Long gone."

Yes, Liam would be long gone, and Cian would be alone for the first time since he was two years old.

**

Katya had slept through much of the morning, and when she woke, they were in a cheap motel room with an expressway outside the small window.

"Hey." Liam came walking out of the bathroom, hair wet, a towel around his waist.

For one brief moment, Katya was so distracted by the vision of him bare-chested, tattoos covering his shoulders and pecs, that she forgot about Nadja. Then it all came rushing back like a wall of cold, stinging water that plowed into her full blast. She gasped and put a hand to her face, covering her eyes for a moment as she reminded herself to let the breath flow in and out of her lungs.

She felt the weight of the bed shift as Liam sat on the edge. His hand touched hers where it lay over her face.

"It's always hardest first thing in the morning," he told her gently. "There's that second where you forget that the worst thing to ever happen to you has, and then it hits you like a freight train."

She let him pull her hand away, and her gaze met his. His eyes were so kind, so warm and understanding. She didn't know how she'd ever thought he was harsh or cruel or rough. No, Liam MacFarlane was a big, rough man, but he was a loving, gentle one as well. He might break the laws, but he was nothing like the men at the brothel—the men who had tortured and murdered sweet, good Nadja.

"I know it doesn't feel like it," he continued, his thumb stroking the back of her hand over and over. "But it will get easier. Not every morning will feel like this."

"I want to feel this always," she said. "She was worth this. She was worth my sadness every day."

He cupped her face with his other hand, his palm covering her from jawbone to temple, and just watched her while she spoke.

"I never know Nadja's mother, and her father leave many years ago. She grow up with her grandparents. They are poor, and old, but they love her. When she leave to come to America, they think they'll never see her again. She think she would save money and send for them very soon. I never agree— they are old, they do not speak English." She shrugged, and Liam nodded to indicate he understood.

"But now I will tell them…this…" She swallowed to keep the tears at bay. "She was not like me. She was loved."

A fierce expression spread over Liam's face, and he took her face between both of his hands, his voice a rough growl as he leaned close to her. "Don't you ever say you aren't loved. The people in your life may not have been good at showing it, but believe me, no one could know you and not love you, Katerina Volkova."

His kiss was firm, reassuring and unsettling all at once. She made a small sound as he caught her off guard, but when his hand wrapped around the back of her neck, cupping her head like it was the most precious thing in the world, she melted into him, opening to him with her body and her heart.

The heat between them exploded, and in moments, she was flat on the bed, his big body on top of hers, his knee between her legs, and his hands roaming everywhere, one hand on her bare leg beneath her pajama shorts, and the other caressing her breast through the thin cotton of her tank top.

She gasped as everything inside her came alive, and then she remembered Nadja. Nadja, who would never again feel a kind touch. Nadja, who would never again have a friend listen to her sorrows. Nadja, who would never have the freedom Liam had promised to Katya.

As if he could read her mind, Liam stopped, pulling away and watching her carefully.

"I'm sorry," he whispered. "Too fast? Please don't let me do something you don't want. You've been through more than enough."

She smiled at him even as a tear rolled down her face. "And someday, I tell you all that happened. Someday, I will need to tell it, and there is no one who understand better than you. But no, it's not too fast. It's that Nadja will never know this"—she pointed between them—"and that makes me more sad than all the rest."

Liam sighed as he buried his head in her hair alongside her neck. "It makes me sad not just for Nadja," he murmured, caressing her cheek with his. He looked into her eyes. "It makes me sad for everyone who isn't you and isn't me. Because I can't imagine any two people have ever known each other the way we do, and that's beyond sad."

Then he kissed her again, and this time, Liam didn't stop, and Katya didn't think about Nadja or the Bratva or the men who'd bought her in the brothel. She only thought about life, and Liam, and what it meant to understand another human being clear to your very soul.

**

The plan came together overnight. A long night that had Cian, Liam, Lila, and Finn pacing the floor of an expensive hotel suite while Katya sat on the sofa, quietly watching all of them.

Lila felt the tension between Cian and Liam, but she didn't know what to do about it. Cian had told her Liam was leaving, but he'd refused to discuss it with her, and it hurt. His refusal to confide in her made her feel as though he was releasing her alongside his brother.

"At nine thirty, I'll contact Sergei and tell him you're ready to meet," Finn said.

"At ten, we'll get the girl's body into the warehouse where the meeting is set." Finn glanced at

Katya with an apology.

"We'll be out by ten fifteen. Your contact sends the feds in immediately after," Liam said from his perch on top of the dining room table where he'd lain down in exhaustion, his six-foot-two frame covering most of the long surface. Cian didn't seem to mind his brother had his steel-toed boots on the glossy black tabletop.

"Louis will be waiting with a boat for us at the dock so we don't risk getting snared on the way out," Finn continued.

"Leaving the Russians to face the feds with Nadja's corpse and the USB drive detailing all their business," Lila finished. She'd been amazed at how easily Finn and Liam had accepted Cian had contacts with access to the FBI. They hadn't questioned him at all, and somehow the possibility he'd been informing never crossed their minds. It frightened her that he could engender so much trust in those who loved him while simultaneously lying to their faces, and it made her wonder if he was playing her the same way every moment they were together.

"Okay, how does it go from there?" Cian spun his finger in the air to indicate they needed to keep rehearsing.

"Louis takes us to the airfield, where Jimmy will have Katya waiting with the plane and the paperwork," Finn said.

Lila watched Cian's face and saw the way he flinched when Finn mentioned the word airfield.

"Katya and I get on a plane, and Finn tells everyone we were still there when the Russians and the feds showed up and I was shot as we escaped to the boat. Then he tossed me overboard when I bled out, I'm dead at the bottom of the lake, and no one can look for me because we can't admit I was there in the first place."

Lila's stomach clenched thinking about how devastated Mrs. MacFarlane would undoubtedly be thinking one of her sons was dead. She'd never met the woman, but surely any mother would be permanently destroyed by the death of a child.

"Are you sure there isn't some way to tell your mother the truth?" Lila asked. "It seems so…cruel…"

Cian pinched his nose and closed his eyes. "It *is* cruel, and if there was another way, I'd take it, but if anyone knows Liam is alive, the Russians will never stop. I can't risk someone noticing my Ma's not adequately upset. The Bratva are notorious for their patience when it comes to revenge. Waiting ten or more years is nothing to them. They'll go Liam Neeson on Liam MacFarlane. If we *could* ask Ma, she'd tell us to hurt her if it meant saving her son."

Lila nodded, discomfort still making her stomach squirm. It was a decent plan—lure the Russians into taking a fall. Leave them with their dead body and a USB drive full of illegal Russian accounts and activities. The MacFarlanes would be in the clear, the Russians would have lost—for now—and Liam and Katya would be free. But there were a lot of "ifs" in the plan.

Finn sighed from the armchair he'd flopped on ten minutes earlier. "The real beauty of this is that in addition to any arrests for the murder, the Russians will get so much scrutiny from the feds, they'll have to close up shop here. If they try to expand into Chicago again, it'll be years from now."

And Lila knew enough about Cian's long-term

plans to realize he wouldn't be around in years. He'd be dead or in prison. Because that was all the man thought he was worth, and it broke her heart to learn it.

"Okay," Cian said. "I think we all need to get some sleep."

"Yep, I just have to bring some nose plugs over to the guys guarding the corpse first…" Finn's voice faded as he glanced at Katya and grimaced.

"Finn!" Cian reprimanded sharply. "A little respect."

Liam played the faux pas off casually, walking by Finn's chair and slapping him on the shoulder. "You're disgusting, dude," he quipped before rounding the chair to reach for Katya's hand and pull her up from the sofa. He put an arm around her shoulders. "While you're playing with dead bodies, we're going to get some sleep. These days, I never know when I'll have another chance."

Cian nodded at Liam, and Lila watched a look pass between them.

"We have men at every entry to the newest safehouse," Cian said quietly to Finn. "But I'm still worried. It's been too long since their last move."

Finn stood. "I trust your gut, but this time, I think it's wrong. Lila sending that false building inspection work order for their brothel meant they'd have to move all those girls—fast. That could have easily taken them the last day and a half. My guess is they won't be back to normal business until tonight at the earliest. And maybe not until tomorrow. I think we can relax until tomorrow morning, and by then, the meeting will be set."

Cian grunted, his brow still furrowed. "Okay, but

take an extra guy or two and stay alert."

Finn acquiesced and left the suite.

Cian turned to Lila. "You ready to go home?" he asked.

And it struck her that she'd taken to thinking of it that way—his condo—home. She'd been spending her nights in Cian's bed and her days in his office hacking Russian accounts, stealing their money, hiding information they needed. In a matter of days, she'd settled into a routine, and it felt...comfortable. Working with Cian had felt that way since the beginning. Yes, she'd been nervous because of his reputation, but when they talked about work—the real nuts and bolts of how to do what he needed—it had been comfortable. They understood each other, and it made the problem solving that much easier.

But in bed together they were something far beyond comfortable. Something unique that could only be created by the two of them. They weren't Lila and Cian then; they were something new, something transcendent. And she knew it was all about to end. She'd felt it ever since he'd told her Liam was going to run. She'd sensed it in the distant look in his eyes and the careful way he'd held her the night before. Lila knew she was about to lose not only her home, but the man she'd come to love.

"Sure," she told him with a falsely cheerful smile. His response was a grimace, but then he walked to her and pulled her into an embrace.

"I'm sorry," he whispered. "For all of this. I'm sorry you're involved, I'm sorry you're in danger." He kissed her forehead.

"I'm here because I want to be." *Please don't make me go,* she thought.

He just gazed at her, his face an array of emotions and thoughts, things she knew he wouldn't share, but she could glean anyway. Then he took her hand and led her out of the hotel. Once they got to his condo, he undressed her carefully and made love to her with such tenderness, Lila thought her heart might truly break in two. He was saying goodbye, and she didn't know how to stop him.

Chapter Sixteen

Cian watched the light fade outside the plateglass windows of his condo. The sun was nearly down, and the clock was ticking. He could hear Lila clacking away on the computer in his office, where she'd been holed up all afternoon. Things were tense between them, and he didn't like it but also couldn't seem to help it.

He feared if he started talking to her, he'd never stop. She had that quietness about her, a patient way of listening, and really hearing everything he said. If he told her how terrified he was of being without Liam again, he might not be able to stop the torrent of words and emotions. He might not be able to keep from telling her how much he loved her and that losing her and Liam at the same time was going to be the death of him. He'd planned for this, chosen it, wanted it—and he still did—but damn, it was hard.

He turned away from the windows and went to the bar, pouring out a generous portion of

Connemara for himself and a glass of Merlot for Lila. Then he made his way into the office.

Lila looked up when he walked in, and her eyes still had that slightly glazed look they got when she was so deep in coding she sometimes didn't blink for what seemed like minutes.

"Hey," he said, smiling at her rosy cheeks and messy hair. She'd climbed out of bed and gone straight to the computer, so she was still in yoga pants and a tank top with no bra. His favorite Lila outfit.

"Is that for me?" She pointed to the wineglass.

"Yeah, you able to take a break?"

"Yes." She hit one key before standing. "I was actually working on Rogue business. I've been neglecting it with everything else we're doing."

He nodded and handed her the wine as she came around the desk. He led the way back to the living room, and soon they were both seated on the sofa, her legs curled under her like she always did, his whiskey already half gone.

He set his tumbler on the coffee table, resting his elbows on his spread knees. "We need to talk about what happens after tonight," he said, his voice rough.

He glanced at her, and she just stared at him with those big, dark, soulful eyes.

"If this works, the Russians will be under control for a while. I'll have to play the part of grieving brother—"

"I don't think that's going to be such a stretch for you," she said softly.

He looked at her again and gave her a twisted smile. Yes, she already knew. He didn't even need to say it.

"True." Then he took a deep breath and let it

out. "I told you I want my brothers out, safe, free from all this. I'll only have Finn left, and I know I can make a deal with the feds—a trade—me for him. I'll give them my dad, the business, and me, and then it will all be over."

Her mouth formed an O of surprise, and he plunged on before she could respond.

"I plan to do it fast. I've already given them things on the business, and what I've been holding back will seal it. I'll get immunity for Finn, and they can have the rest, including me."

A tear ran down Lila's face, but he didn't reach out to brush it away, just kept going, sticking to the business at hand like he had so many times before.

"Once the funeral for Liam is over, I'll go to them. So maybe as soon as a week from now. I hate having to do it to my Mom, but maybe if Finn has immunity, he can be with her, help her through it all."

Then he sat up and turned to face her full-on. He grabbed her hand in both of his and squeezed it as the tears continued to trickle silently down her face.

"You have to go—tonight. I want you out of this, away from any blowback from the Russians, any fallout with the police. When I let the feds have the information on my organization, it will lead them to your business, and you can't be in the country when that happens."

She didn't say a word, just nodded, the tears coming faster.

"Lila from Rogue." His voice was ragged with pain. "Knowing you has been—" He paused, not sure if he had the words to convey what he felt. "A privilege. I never thought I would get the chance to fall in love."

Her gaze jumped to his, and he smiled warmly at her. "But then you came along, and you made the impossible possible. I can never thank you enough for that."

She sobbed then, just once, and it tore open something inside of him that he didn't think would ever heal.

"I'm going to the airstrip to make sure everything's ready. Then I'll wait for Liam to arrive so I can say goodbye. I need you to get your things together while I'm gone and go to the car. You remember where it's parked?"

"Yes," she whispered, her eyes pleading with him to stop. But he couldn't. It was now or never, and he had to do what was best for her. What would give her a long and happy life.

"Danny will take you there. Tell him where to go, then follow the instructions in the glove box. You'll leave from a different airfield from the one Liam will be at. Don't talk to anyone, not even your mother, I'll take care of her. Promise me."

"I promise."

He gazed at her for a moment, breathing in her scent, absorbing the feel of her skin, memorizing the planes of her face.

"I will fund an account for your mom—"

"I already did." Lila gave him a sad smile.

Of course she did. He chuckled. "Good. Now listen, I know you can find a way to contact me once you're there, but don't. No matter how good you are, it's too much of a risk. No one can ever know where you went. You heard what I said about the Russians? They won't stop."

"Okay."

"Come here." He pulled her into his arms and held her as close as he could, his heart beating so fast, it felt like he'd just fought twelve rounds. Her soft hair tickled his skin, and then he pulled back just enough to kiss her sweet lips, refraining from anything more than a quick brush because he knew he'd undo all of it if he gave in for even a moment.

"Goodbye, Lila," he murmured, looking into her eyes. Then he stood and walked to the door. Keeping himself from turning to look back at her was the hardest thing he'd ever done.

**

An hour later, Lila stood in the foyer of Cian's apartment and looked around one last time. She doubted she'd ever see the place again, and she wanted to commit it to memory. The kitchen where she'd first seen him shirtless, the living room where he'd made love to her against the glass that took up one whole wall, the office where she'd penetrated nearly every cyber wall the Russians had.

No, she wouldn't see this place again, but she damn well would see the man she loved again. She'd promised she wouldn't contact him, and she'd stick to that, but she hadn't promised she wouldn't help him. She could, and she would. She wasn't going to allow him to sacrifice himself while everyone else walked away—even if walking away was done under phony names in the dead of night on chartered planes to corrupt islands with no extradition.

She looked down at the envelope in her hand with Cian's name written on it. She didn't know what it meant, didn't know if it was a legitimate danger or not, but she couldn't leave without telling him what she'd seen on his father's security cameras. The last thing she wanted was to believe Danny could be betraying Cian. Danny was Cian's man. And, she had to admit—hers. He was the guard who'd been there from the first time Cian had insisted she needed protection all the way until tonight. He was the one who'd drive her to the car that Cian had left for her. The car that would take her to the new life Cian paid for.

She didn't want to believe Danny was disloyal, but she couldn't leave Cian without alerting him to the possibility. So she laid the envelope on the foyer table, then opened the door.

"You all set?" Danny asked where he stood waiting in the hallway.

"Yes." She tried to smile at him, but her heart wasn't in it.

He squeezed her shoulder sympathetically. "You know he wants you safe, right?"

She nodded as they made their way to the elevator.

"We all do." He smiled at her, and once again, she couldn't believe he would betray his boss. He loved Cian, and he'd been nothing but kind to her.

"I know. Thank you for everything you've done for me."

"Sure thing," he told her as they descended to the parking garage. "Stay right here," he ordered as he stepped out of the elevator, gun in hand, and looked around the area. When he was satisfied it was all clear, he led her to one of Cian's SUVs and helped her inside. He'd had the building's concierge take her bags down earlier.

They pulled out of the garage from the back entrance, Danny keeping a watchful eye all around them as he drove. His phone pinged with a text, but he waited until they got to a stoplight before he pulled it from his pocket to look. Lila saw his brow furrow as he read it, but then he shrugged and replaced it in his pocket.

"I need to make a stop before I take you to the garage," he told her. "Boss needs something."

"Cian?" she asked, worried something had gone wrong with the plan.

"Nah, the big boss, Mr. MacFarlane."

Lila's chest went cold.

"I'm sure it won't take long. He usually just has some question he wants answered or an errand he needs run."

"Doesn't he have his own guys to do that stuff?" she asked, the back of her neck tingling in warning.

Danny glanced at her and shifted uncomfortably. "Yeah, but we used to switch around more. I worked for him before I ever worked for Cian."

Lila just nodded, discomfort rising the longer they drove.

Fifteen minutes later, they arrived at the electronic gates to Robbie MacFarlane's property. Danny opened the window and punched a code he obviously knew by heart onto the keypad. Then the gates swung open and they pulled forward, up a short drive to a roundabout that spanned the front of the large brick house.

As they arrived, two of Robbie's men came to the car, one opening the driver's door and the other Lila's.

"Danny," said the first man. "Mr. Mac wants you

to help me with the choice about what glass to have put in his new car."

"It couldn't wait till morning?" Danny asked, seeming genuinely confused.

"You know how he gets," the other man answered, leading Danny away from the car. "He doesn't have enough to do, so stuff like this becomes an emergency."

Danny stopped. Turned to look toward Lila.

"I'll take her inside, and Mrs. MacFarlane will get her a cup of tea or something while you do that," the second man said as he put a hand on Lila's elbow. Everything in her screamed that something wasn't right, and Danny looked like he'd been blindsided, unsure whether to follow Lila or the man on his left, who hovered, tense and impatient.

"She needs to stay with me—" Danny began, but the first man interrupted him.

"He's got her. She's just going to be in the kitchen. Let's hurry and do this so the old man can go to bed and you can get back to business."

Before he could look back to her, Lila was in motion, the second man's hand on her elbow almost painfully tight. She jerked her arm to try to get him to release her, but then there was a gun pressing to her side, and she knew her instincts had been dead-on.

It was dark, the only lights those that illuminated the drive and yard of the MacFarlane mansion. Danny was being distracted by the other man, and her new captor leaned down and whispered, "Don't say a word, and no one will get hurt. Try to involve Danny, and we'll have to kill him."

Lila swallowed and did as she was told.

The man propelled her into the house, taking a

sharp left at the entrance before walking her down a long hallway. He stopped at the last door and opened it. It led to the back parking area of the compound where there were no lights, only the moon that provided a faint gray glow to the gravel parking area and the big black Lincoln Town Car that waited in the center.

Somehow, Lila knew if she got into that car, she might never get out. She began to struggle, trying to remember the moves Cian had taught her at Sean O'Neil's gym all those months ago. She also realized she didn't even have her purse with the gun he'd given her. It sat in the car on the other side of the property, useless as hell.

The man dug the gun into her side harder as she tried to wrench her arm from his grip.

"Don't do that now. I don't want to hurt you," he said softly. "You won't be able to get away. Just cooperate, and maybe the old man will let you go after he talks to you."

Her heart raced, and she held her body stiff as the man practically dragged her the remainder of the way. At the car waited another of Robbie's men, and he opened the door as her captor shoved her in. The door was shut, and the locks clicked into place within a fraction of a second. The engine started, and they were moving before Lila even had a chance to turn and look into the same icy blue eyes the man she loved possessed.

"Hello," Robbie said. "We meet again."

**

Robbie watched the girl as she glared at him from the

corner of the backseat.

"Now, now," he soothed. "No need to be upset. No one's going to hurt you, I just need you to take my hospitality for a few days while I discipline my boys a bit. They're young, and I'm afraid I spoiled them. Sometimes leverage is the only tool a parent has." He smiled, and noticed her cringe as she looked at him.

"Where are you taking me?"

Robbie watched the shadowy scenery go by outside the tinted windows. "Not far," he answered.

"He'll find me, you know."

"Oh, I'm sure he'll try, but he's never been able to outsmart me. Now won't be the time he does."

The pretty hacker laughed at him, and Robbie felt his anger flare to life.

"He's never been able to outsmart you? Have you seen Connor lately?"

He was livid now, but kept his composure as they neared the road where they needed to turn off. He waited, not responding, not giving her any clue as to what was coming next. He could see her smug expression turn to fear as the last few minutes of their journey ticked by.

Then they were pulling up to the perfect spot to store a disobedient employee like Lila.

When the car finally stopped, Robbie leaned toward her. "I know it wasn't Cian who hid my son from me." He laced his words with menace. "He never could have done it without you, and now I'm going to make sure you understand what happens to people who take something that's mine."

**

214

Lila felt bile rise in her throat as she stared at Robbie and the sick smile that cut across his face. But before she could answer him, the door next to her opened, and a hand wrapped around her upper arm.

That was when she panicked, kicking and screaming, arms flying, feet scrabbling for purchase against her assailant's attack. She felt her leg scrape against the ground as she was pulled from the car, and then she heard Robbie's voice. "She's got more fire than my son. Do what you have to."

A beefy arm wrapped around her throat, and Lila's mind flashed back to the day Xavier Rossi held her windpipe in his hand, crushing the life out of her. She brought an elbow back hard into the assailant's gut, and he loosened his hold just a touch, giving her all the room she needed to get her teeth bared and bite down hard on his forearm. She tasted blood just as she heard him shout, "Bitch!" Then she was whirled around while he held on to her upper arm. She didn't recognize the man, but his face was a mask of fury as he shook out his wounded arm.

"Get control of her," she heard Robbie instruct before his footsteps echoed away across gravel and dried grass.

"Gladly," the man holding her said. He threw her against the side of the car, the door handle jamming into her lower back and sending a shockwave of pain up her spine.

"You need to keep your teeth to yourself," he snarled before backhanding her across the cheek.

Her eyes watered, and she tasted blood again, this time from her own mouth. She lifted her knee, intending to nail him in the balls, but he was too fast, grabbing her leg and pulling her so she fell onto the ground hard, her head bouncing off the dirt, pieces of gravel lodging in her scalp.

And that was when she realized what was about to happen. She saw it coming, and knew she'd lost. No matter how hard she fought, these men would beat her—in every sense of the word. She thought about Cian and what he'd tried to teach her, about how worried he'd been for her safety these last few months, how he'd kept her guarded every moment, day and night. She thought about how he'd tried to explain to her his world was one of no forgiveness, no mercy. But even Cian hadn't understood that no matter what he did, the biggest threat of all came from inside his own house, his own family. She didn't think Cian had any idea that the man who would finally get them all was his own father.

So Lila watched as the man hired by Robbie MacFarlane drew back his foot and swung at her head.

**

Cian got the summons from his father while he was waiting at the airport for Liam to arrive. It was almost time for Liam and Finn to set the plan in motion, and the last thing he needed was to hear his father's bullshit. But when a second text came demanding he respond immediately, he knew he was going to have to report. The quicker he took care of whatever his father wanted, the sooner he'd be able to get back to handling the real business of the night.

Fifteen minutes later, he climbed out of his car,

telling the driver to stay close, they wouldn't be there long. He strode into the house, noticing most of the lights were off. His mother must already be in bed, which was good because he didn't have a lot of patience for his father this evening. If they came to blows, it was better she wasn't around to see it.

He'd started down the hallway to his father's office when he heard the old man's voice from the living room. Cian turned and walked into the darkened room, where Robbie sat nursing a glass of whiskey.

"Have a seat," Robbie instructed.

Fuck. Cian did not have time for this.

"I'll stand," he answered. "What do you need?"

Robbie chuckled, and Cian's muscles tensed.

"I wanted you to be here for the show," Robbie said. "It's going to be lots of fun, and I wouldn't want you to miss it."

"What the hell are you talking about?" Cian asked, crossing his arms and widening his stance.

Robbie stood and began to amble slowly around the room. "I think you neglected to tell me something...son."

Cian's eyes narrowed.

"About a little meeting you have set up this evening?"

Cian managed not to blink. "I figured I'd tell you after we had the Russians all cleaned up and out of the way," Cian said.

"Mm-hmm," Robbie murmured. "It's not the Russians I'm thinking about."

Cian's hand clenched involuntarily.

"Because here's the thing, I think if this little meeting were just about the Russians, you would have told me what you were up to. It's what happens after the Russians are tidied up that you didn't want me to know."

"What are you talking about?" Cian asked, his mind racing for a way out of this.

"I'm talking about you running off another of your brothers."

Cian had no options but full disclosure. He braced himself. "He needs to get away from the Bratva. They're not going to stop hunting him."

"Then he shouldn't have taken the whore in the first place." Robbie's voice was deadly cold.

Cian's head hammered. "But he did, so now we have to do what we need to to keep him safe."

Robbie tossed back the rest of his whiskey, then slammed it down on the nearest hard surface, which happened to be Cian's mother's prized grand piano. "No son of mine will run like a fucking pussy. He started this. He'll end it. He'll stay and fight like a man."

"And no brother of mine will be used as live bait to start a war we have no chance of winning," Cian answered, taking a step toward Robbie.

Robbie pulled his phone out of his pocket and looked at the time. "We'll see about that," he said, swiping the screen and punching numbers.

He put it on speaker as the phone began to ring, and Cian moved toward him again, but this time, the old man pulled a gun from his waistband and gestured at Cian with it. "I wouldn't if I were you," he said.

The phone call connected, and Cian heard a voice on the other end say, "That you, Robbie?"

Cian stared at his father, frozen with confusion

and rage and some sort of misplaced idea that he couldn't *actually* take the old man down, no matter what Robbie might be up to.

"Officer O'Brian" Robbie said congenially as Cian's heart sank. O'Brian was his father's favorite inside man in the CPD. "I have that tip I was telling you about. You'll want to go to warehouse four. You'll find two men and a dead body there. You'll want to arrest them both. They've been hiding that corpse for several days, and they're involved in all manner of illegal activities."

"Well," said the officer on the other end of the line, "thank you so much for that information. I'll pass on this *anonymous* tip right away and have all the cars in the area head there now."

Robbie smiled, then disconnected the call.

"They have a way out, you know," Cian told him, his heart racing in spite of his determination not to panic.

Robbie chuckled again.

"You mean the boat that Louis will have waiting?"

And that was when Cian knew his brothers were screwed. And also that someone had betrayed him to his father.

"Yeah," Robbie continued. "Louis won't be there. I have him helping out with a little something for me."

Cian didn't hesitate, merely reached into his jacket pocket and pulled out his phone. Robbie raised the gun.

"Go ahead," Cian said, hardly sparing him a glance. "Then explain to my mother how it happened."

Robbie hesitated, and Cian took the chance, pressing the speed dial for Liam. Robbie watched him as he did it.

Liam answered on the first ring, and before he could even say hello, Cian growled one word.

"Run."

Chapter Seventeen

Liam stared at the phone in his hand. Cian had said one word, then disconnected, and it was taking Liam a moment to process it. A moment that was one too many, apparently, as the distant sound of sirens came rushing to his consciousness.

"Fuck!" he snapped, shoving the phone in his pocket. "Someone tipped the cops off. We have to go!"

Finn frantically tried to stuff the USB drive in Nadja's hand. The corpse hadn't been kept on ice, and it wouldn't be long before bloat set in. It was also still partially in rigor mortis, and Finn struggled to open the clenched fingers.

"Forget that," Liam commanded, cursing his brother's insistence on the details of things. "We have to go—now."

They heard the scattering of gravel as police cars peeled to a halt in front of the building.

"Go!" Finn yelled, and followed as Liam started

running for the back door that would lead them to the docks and the waiting boat.

They skidded to a stop at the back door, trying to listen even as they heard police crashing through the front of the building.

"We've got one body!" someone shouted. "Fan out. They can't be far!"

"Let's hope they're not out back," Liam muttered before he pushed on the door. It protested, and Liam cursed before elbowing Finn back so he could kick the damn thing open.

As his foot made contact with the metal and the door ripped open, he heard someone shout, "Hands up! Don't move!" Liam looked over his shoulder as he saw Finn's arms lift into the air. *No. No. No.*

Liam froze, Finn's body in front of him, screening him from the police, the door—and freedom—behind him.

"Go," Finn said so softly only Liam could hear him.

"Never," Liam answered, reaching into his waistband to remove his gun.

"Yes," Finn murmured. "I've got this. Take your chance, and your girl, and go."

Time slowed to a stop, and Liam stood, gun in hand, faced with the hardest choice of his life. Run. Fight. Or give up.

He'd been a fighter most of his life. A role he'd taken on voluntarily, a part he'd played to make sure his brother and his father didn't kill each other. And it had taken its toll on him. Had made him a man he wasn't sure he was always proud of. It had also made him a survivor. He could live through anything—but did he want to?

He didn't, and that was why giving up wasn't an option. Could he survive prison again? Yeah. But he'd rather die.

So now he had to decide—be the fighter he always had been, or leave and become someone new, someone a little kinder, a little gentler, and maybe a little happier as well. He loved his brothers. The last thing he wanted to do was leave them in this mess. It terrified him to think of Finn in prison, but he wasn't sure he could keep being the man they'd come to expect from him.

Now he was a man who had someone else who needed him. Someone who thought he was more than an enforcer, more than a cold-blooded killer. Someone who'd forgiven him even when he left her to be tortured and raped. He owed Cian his life, but he owed Katya his humanity.

And right now, he owed Finn his respect, because the brother he'd thought couldn't handle the worst of who they were was telling Liam that he did, in fact, have what it took.

"*Slán abhaile*," Finn whispered as the cop began yelling instructions about getting on the floor.

"*Slán abhaile*," Liam repeated, his heart a swollen rock inside his chest.

Then he ran.

**

Liam's breath came in quick huffs as he waited inside the brothel. He knew the Russians would be returning soon since the meeting place was now crawling with cops. He'd managed to make his way through the labyrinth of warehouses and docks until he found a parking garage, where he'd hotwired an old pickup truck and driven straight here. Time was running short, and he hadn't yet stopped to grab a phone and call Cian, but he had one last task to complete before he left town, and he was damned if he was going to skip it.

He saw the dark sedan pull up and felt all his instincts kick in at once. He waited quietly in the small, dank room as he watched through the window while Sergei climbed from the car.

One of the men with Sergei exited as well, while the other one sped off in the car. Once the men had entered the building, Liam turned his attention to listening to the sounds below. He'd come in on the second floor, a different window, but same general area as when he'd first found Katya.

He could hear orders being shouted in Russian on the floor below him and wished he had Katya's knowledge of the language so he knew what they were saying. They probably assumed the MacFarlanes had been arrested and were preparing to celebrate.

"Not on my watch," he murmured to himself.

It took him almost ten minutes to make his way down the stairs and into the long hallway that ran the width of the building. As he slid along the corridor, the sounds of voices got closer. Most of the doors looked exactly the same, and he knew they held rooms like the one he'd been placed in when he came looking to purchase "a thin blonde" for the night.

But then he saw one that had a padlock on the outside. He didn't hesitate, pulling out his lockpicking kit and popping the simple lock open in moments. When he swung the door open, the light from the hallway lit the room. Staring back at him with dead eyes were about ten young women, disheveled, exhausted, some of them high, others nearly catatonic. A few gasped as he stood in the doorway watching them.

All he could see was Katya and Nadja, and he knew this moment would define them all for the rest of their lives.

He quietly pulled the door shut behind him, then took out his wallet, extracting a few hundred dollars and a business card.

"Here," he said, holding out the items to the nearest woman.

She stared at him, not responding, not moving.

"Do any of you speak English?" he asked.

"I do," answered a woman from the back of the room.

"This is enough money to get all of you to safety. Go to a hotel, get only one room, but don't let them see all of you. Then call the number on this card. Ask for Cian, tell him Liam gave you the number. Tell him you were being held with Katya. He'll find a way to help you."

The woman who spoke English stood and took the card and the money from him.

"Where are they?" she asked in fear.

"I'm going to handle them. Wait five minutes, then run. Take a left out of this room and head straight down the hall to the exit."

"Why are you doing this?" she asked.

"Because you deserve to be free."

**

A few minutes later, he pulled the silencer out of his pocket and screwed it onto the barrel of the gun. He peeked out the door of the room where the women were kept and saw no one. After making his way down the hall, he turned a corner, and there was the first guard he'd encountered. Before the guy even had a chance to open his mouth, Liam had shot him point-blank in the forehead. The man slumped to the floor, blood running down his face and onto the white dress shirt he wore.

Liam put his ear to the door and heard two voices speaking rapidly in Russian. Once he was satisfied no one else was in the room, he stepped back from the door and knocked loudly once. It swung open, and he repeated the kill tactic by shooting the guy square in the head. As the man's eyes went instantly dead, Liam shoved the body hard before it even had a chance to fall to the floor. He kept a gun in each hand as his gaze tracked rapidly across the room, looking for the other occupant.

"Liam MacFarlane," the accented voice said as Liam's gaze fell on the older man where he stood, pointing his own gun dead center at Liam's chest.

"You must be Sergei," Liam said, stepping farther into the room. "I heard you've been looking for me."

Sergei smiled coldly. "I have. You've stolen something of mine."

Liam kicked the door shut behind him. "That's funny. I didn't think it was possible to have something stolen that never belonged to you."

Sergei nodded slightly. "Be that as it may, I can't have you coming in here all the time and simply taking whatever you fancy."

Liam made a tsking sound. "And I can't have you using humans as possessions in my town. So it appears one of us is going to have to give."

Sergei lifted his gun slightly higher. "I can guarantee it will not be me."

Liam didn't wait, he just shot with both weapons, one winging Sergei's gun hand so his aim was off when he fired the return shot. The other bullet Liam shot was aimed true. It sank into Sergei's chest, and he doubled over, his gun falling from his wounded hand as blood poured from his chest.

Liam walked over and kicked the gun away as Sergei fell to his knees.

The Russian looked up into Liam's eyes, and all Liam saw was hate and misery.

As Sergei knelt before him, Liam thought about Katya, and about all the women who were hopefully escaping to freedom right at that very instant. He thought about what it felt like to be imprisoned, and what Nadja looked like when she was left in that bathtub, cold, and alone, what she must have endured during her final moments.

Then Liam leveled the gun at Sergei's head, waiting as the man's chest continued to bleed while he struggled for breath.

One last time, he thought. "This is for Nadja," he said before he shoved the barrel against Sergei's forehead and pulled the trigger.

**

Cian sat in the backseat of the SUV at the private airfield, his mind a furious buzz after the encounter with his father. Angela had walked in just in time to prevent Cian from killing the old man. But time hadn't played in his favor as he'd raced out of the family compound frantic to reach his brothers before the police did. The hangar next to him was quiet, the jet in front of him was warmed up and ready to go. Jimmy had put Katya on board an hour ago, and now they waited. Finn had been arrested, and Cian had the family lawyers working to get him out. But Liam had escaped, only no one knew how or where. He hadn't heard from his brother in two hours, and his head hurt almost as much as his chest.

His driver's phone pinged. "Looks like we got someone coming into the gate," the man said. "On a motorcycle."

Cian sat up, leaning forward to look out the front windshield. There were two other MacFarlane SUVs there, and they had formed a line in front of the broadside of the plane. As the motorcycle came closer, MacFarlane men emerged from the other two SUVs and took up positions of protection, automatic weapons at the ready. The driver of Cian's car opened the door and did the same.

But Cian knew none of it was necessary, because he could already tell that the motorcyclist was his brother. The man was indestructible, and Cian couldn't believe he'd worried at all.

He climbed out of the car and waved his arm for the men to lower their weapons. Liam cruised up and came to a stop right in front of him, a grin on his face a mile wide.

Cian couldn't help but smile back. "Nice ride," he said.

"It got the job done. The guy that left it sitting

outside the rail station on Van Buren Street after dark was an idiot. It was begging to get stolen."

Cian shook his head as Liam climbed off and yanked a wire that disconnected the engine of the Ducati.

"They got Finn," Liam said, sobering immediately.

"I know. But I had a lawyer there before they even got him through booking." He put a hand on Liam's shoulder. "He's going to be okay."

Liam ran a hand over his buzz-cut hair, then rubbed the stubble on his jaw. "I left him there. He told me to go but…"

"It's better one of you out than both of you in," Cian answered. And it was true. He had what he needed to get Finn freed. If Liam had been locked up it may very well have been for life.

"I want to know how the hell the cops knew to come," Liam said. "Did the Russians figure us out?"

Had it been Finn or Connor, Cian wouldn't have told the truth. He would have continued to protect them like he had their whole lives, letting them believe that while their father might not be an easy man, he wasn't a monster.

But Liam already knew. He'd seen the very worst of their father at a very young age, and Cian knew that telling him the truth now would ensure Liam got on that plane and never looked back. And as much as Cian's heart would break when that happened, it did need to happen.

"It was Pop," Cian said, moving Liam farther from the men who stood waiting for instructions on what to do next.

"What?"

"One of the guys obviously told him our plan. He knew we had the meeting and knew you were going to jet. He decided he'd rather have you in prison than anywhere else."

Liam's face stiffened, and his fists clenched. Cian watched him struggle to contain his anger.

"Hey," he said, a hand on Liam's shoulder. "You knew this about him already. Nothing's changed. But now you know—you can't ever come back."

Nodding, Liam expelled a long breath. "Yep. Got the message—loud and clear."

They looked into each other's eyes then, and it all passed between them—the hurt, the shock, the death of their childhoods. Robbie had taken something from each of them that night, and they'd been looking for it ever since. Cian could only hope that with Katya and a fresh start, Liam would finally find it again.

"What will happen to you now?" Liam asked, his voice low.

"Don't worry about it, I have plans."

Liam smiled sadly. "You always do."

"Your woman's onboard waiting for you. I imagine she's getting tired of Jimmy's company by now."

Liam chuckled. "He's probably gotten her to play that stupid game with the animal names."

Cian shrugged. "Probably. Maybe it's kept her mind off worrying." He reached into his inside jacket pocket. "Here's the paperwork. I've already told the pilot the destination, and there'll be a car waiting to take you to the property I bought."

"Jesus. You didn't have to do all that."

"Yeah, I did. There may come a day when that place is no longer safe, but at least you'll have somewhere to land until you get adjusted. You and Katya barely know each other. I thought you could do with a little honeymoon."

Liam snorted. "A honeymoon, huh?"

Cian wrapped his hand around the back of Liam's neck and pulled them together, foreheads touching. "Live for us both," he said. "*Slán abhaile.*"

Liam was quiet for a moment, as they stood there breathing each other's air. "*Slán abhaile,*" he answered.

Then Cian pushed his brother away, gave him a slap on the back, and walked to the car.

**

It was nearly two hours into the flight before Liam finally woke up. He and Katya had simply curled around each other on the reclining seat of the small jet and fallen asleep. Now, he looked outside to see nothing but darkness, and wondered what the time zone difference would be when they landed.

He tucked Katya closer, burying his nose in her soft hair, breathing in the scent of freedom. There had been a few moments there—when he'd discovered there was no Louis and no boat—when he'd thought he wasn't going to make it. He'd left strict instructions with Cian and Jimmy that if something went wrong, they were to force Katya to leave without him. But damn, he was glad he'd made it with her.

"What are you thinking?" she asked sleepily. He looked down at her soft gaze and couldn't stop himself from kissing her plush lips.

"About how happy I am to be here with you."

She smiled. "Good. It makes me happy too."

They were both quiet for a moment, the hum of the jet's engines creating a white noise around them.

"So," Liam began, not sure how to express what he wanted to say. "My brother got us all set up. When we get there, he has a house for us, money, the whole nine yards."

"This is good, yes?" Katya asked. "We can stay in one place? Not move around?"

"Yes, it is."

"So why you have this line"—she traced the skin between his eyes—"here? You worry why?"

He took her finger and kissed it before placing her hand back on his chest where he liked it. "Cian said something before I got on board. He said he got us the house because he thought we deserved a honeymoon."

Katya waited, one eyebrow raised in question.

"Is that what you want?" he finally asked. "Do you want to stay with me if we're finally safe? Would you want to actually...*marry* me?" God, he couldn't believe he was even thinking stuff like this, much less saying it.

Katya blinked at him for a moment, then a smile curved her lips, and he thought he'd never seen a woman look so feline in his life.

"I think someday you will ask me this when we live together for a time. I leave cap off toothpaste or cook bad Russian food you might not want me."

"Oh no, you don't," he told her, pulling her on top of him so she had to look him in the eye. "There's nothing you could do that would turn me off. I told you that. I grew up with three brothers and a father who's a son of a bitch. Nothing grosses me out. Nothing scares me away."

She smiled bigger. "Then someday when you feel like it, you ask me the question again...and I will say yes."

Liam didn't have any more words after that. He was a man of action, after all, and Katya was going to be his favorite activity from now on.

Chapter Eighteen

Lila opened her eyes to a blinding white light. She groaned and screwed them shut again, rolling to her side.

Gradually, the throbbing pain in her temples subsided, and she cracked one eye open again. She was lying on a small bed, not unlike what they might give you in prison. Beneath the bed was a concrete floor. Next to it, pointed directly at her, was that horrible bright light she wanted to shatter, and across the room was a metal door, one small window opening in it.

She sat up gingerly, taking stock of her physical condition, and concluding that aside from what felt to be a concussion and a face that felt swollen to the point of numbness, nothing else seemed hurt.

"Well," said a voice with a heavy brogue from the corner. "I can see why the boy likes you. You are quite lovely in your exotic way, aren't ya?"

Lila's heart jumped, and she gasped as she

realized someone else was in the room with her. She looked to the corner, and a man leaned forward from where he sat on a metal folding chair, resting his elbows on his knees. He was trim and probably in his fifties, his fair skin crinkled around light eyes, and his hair a mixture between red and gray.

She swallowed and waited for him to speak again.

"Name's Michael Riley," he said politely. "I'll be your jailer during your stay. Do as you're told, and everything will go fine. Resist like you did when you arrived here, and you'll get more than a knock to the head. Are we clear?"

She nodded, her throat and tongue feeling thick.

"Good." He stood, looking at her with a cold smile. Then he rubbed his cock through his jeans with one hand. "As I said, behave, and you'll be fine. Resist, and maybe I'll take the opportunity to find out more about what Cian sees in you."

After he walked out, Lila lay back down on the cot and shook so hard, her teeth chattered.

**

Cian went straight from the airport to the offices of Maguire, Albrecht, and Phillips, Attorneys at Law. It was past midnight by the time Thomas Maguire, Jr. arrived to meet him.

"I'm sorry you had to wait," Thomas said as he walked into the conference room his secretary had gotten out of bed to open for Cian. He nodded to the guards at the door and sat down across the table. Thomas Maguire Jr. was the son of the original namesake of the firm. Around Cian's age, with auburn hair and green eyes, he was wearing a suit at one a.m., and Cian wondered if the guy had still been in it when he'd gotten the call to go defend Finn.

"How is he?" Cian asked, exhaustion taking a backseat to worry for Finn.

"He's holding up just fine, and I have a bail hearing set for first thing tomorrow morning with Judge Patterson, who tends to be lenient on these things."

"Good. And what about his accommodation right now? There are several groups, one in particular, who might try to get at him in the next few hours."

Thomas had obviously foreseen that. "Yes, and I explained to the feds who showed up in the middle of the interview that if they really wanted a crack at their big-time case, they'd make sure my client was still alive by morning. He's been given a solo cell, and the feds left one of their own to watch him. They don't trust the locals, but there's going to be some infighting over jurisdiction."

Cian snorted. "I'll bet there is."

"Something else that might make you feel better…"

Cian nodded for him to continue.

"About an hour ago, the police found the bodies of Sergei Petrov, Viktor Castrov, and a man named Alexei Nicovich. All Russian mob."

Cian blinked at him. Then he thought about those two hours Liam was missing, and the fact it only took twenty minutes to get from the warehouse where Finn was arrested to the airstrip Cian had waited at. His brother had protected them all to the very end. He shook his head, a small smile coming to his lips.

"I take it you know those names?" Thomas

asked.

"Let's just say I feel a little better about my brother being incarcerated tonight," Cian answered. Thomas simply nodded.

"Can I ask you something?" Thomas said.

Cian waited. In his experience, that was a rhetorical question and didn't require a response.

"My father's been your family's attorney for the last two decades. Why did you call me?"

Cian mulled it over for only a moment. He had neither the time nor the energy to screw around right now. Thomas Jr. didn't know it, but Cian was going to require his assistance a lot in the next few weeks. Cian had to make a decision—trust the man or find someone else. He decided to trust him.

"How serious are you about attorney-client privilege?" Cian asked as he leaned his arms on the conference table.

"Very," Thomas answered. "It's not my problem what my clients may or may not have done. It's my job to represent them to the best of my ability, to protect their interests, and in order to do that, I need to have completely open and confidential discussions with them. I'll go to jail before I'll violate that privilege."

"Good," Cian answered decisively. "Then consider me your client as of now, in addition to Finn. I'll have a second retainer delivered first thing in the morning." He paused. "Your father and mine have been colleagues for a very long time. I called *you* because my father was the one who had my brother arrested this evening."

Thomas's mouth pursed in surprise.

"Okay. So he alerted the police?"

"Yes, he did. And I have no doubt your father would do whatever my father asked him with regard to Finn's case."

Thomas didn't reply to that, but his gaze darkened. "I'm sorry to hear that. You can rest assured that I operate independently of my father."

"I'm counting on it. But I'm also counting on something else. You're going to need to keep any records regarding my brother's case and anything to do with *me* somewhere other than this office. If your father can access the computer systems here, then it's not safe from my father's reach."

"All right," Thomas agreed. "We have a satellite office on the Gold Coast. I can work out of there and keep all the files on an encrypted server housed at that location."

"Good. Give me the address, and I'll have one of my people come out and set up a security system at the office itself."

"I have other clients…"

"As long as you take care of MacFarlane business and do it in a secure location, I don't care what you do with the rest of your time. But my brother has to be your top priority. Above any other client, including me. I'll pay whatever it takes for you to make that happen."

Thomas raised one eyebrow but didn't give any other reaction. "Well then, Mr. MacFarlane, you have yourself a deal."

Cian released a sigh that he'd been holding for what seemed like hours. "Thank you," he answered as he stood. "Is my brother really okay for the next few hours?"

Thomas smiled sympathetically. "Yes, he is, and

honestly, I think your brother was enjoying the whole thing a bit. There was a very attractive female detective that he seemed to take a shine to. My guess is he'll keep himself entertained thinking of ways to aggravate her overnight."

Cian pinched the bridge of his nose. "Jesus," he muttered.

Thomas laughed. "I'll send you the details about the hearing in a few hours when the courts open up."

"Thank you." The two men shook hands, and Cian went down to his car, telling the driver to finally take him home.

**

The penthouse was dark when Cian walked inside. He said goodnight to the guys outside his door and shut it behind him, then stood in the foyer for a moment. He was bone tired, but worried beyond reason. He'd not heard a word from Danny, and all his texts and calls had gone unanswered. He had to know that Lila had gotten away safely. He couldn't understand what Danny could be doing or where he could be. It was unlike him to disappear, and it had Cian on edge.

He went to set his phone on the table in the entry when he saw an envelope in the glow from his screen. He picked it up, preparing to turn on the light and read the contents, but a sound from the living room stopped him. A phone screen flickered on, and Cian nearly jumped out of his skin when he realized Danny was sitting in the dark in his living room.

"What the hell..." Cian moved forward, reaching for the light switch on the wall.

"Please don't," Danny said in a strangled voice.

"I can't face you if I have to do it in the light."

"What's going on?" Cian demanded, dropping the envelope back on the table, panic rising in his gut. "Where is Lila?"

Danny stood, his shadowy form moving across the room until he reached Cian, where he fell to his knees, arms at his sides, his head tipped to the ceiling.

"My God," Cian gasped as his heart leaped to his throat.

"I don't want your mercy," Danny said quietly. "I understand the consequences of what I've done."

"What the fuck *have* you done?" Cian growled, every nerve ending on fire with the anticipation of hearing the one thing he couldn't bear.

"I betrayed you." Danny's voice was rough. "I've been selling you out to your dad—"

Cian moved on impulse, not even realizing he had the other man's collar in his hand until he'd lifted Danny partially off his knees, using the shirt collar to slowly strangle him.

"*You? You* were how he knew about tonight? *You're* the reason Finn is in jail right now?" Cian's voice was like a whip, and Danny struggled, not able to get to his feet, but not able to rest his weight on his knees either.

"Yes. I wanted money. Gambling. I'm sorry. I just thought it was games between you and the old man. I never meant for Lila or anyone else to get involved. I swear I didn't know anyone would actually get hurt. You all like to play games. I thought it was just more of the same old MacFarlane games."

Cian threw the traitor onto his back, then kicked him hard in the gut. Danny coughed and retched for a moment at Cian's feet.

"Stand. Up." Cian's voice was the coldest ice, razor sharp and absolutely deadly.

Danny scrambled to his feet, one arm wrapped around his midsection.

"Where is Lila?"

"I didn't know," Danny gasped. "I swear I had no idea he was going to do it. He called me to come over while I was driving her to the parking garage. He separated us. I never would have left her alone, I'd never have let them take her."

Cian punched him hard in the face. Danny's cheek split, and blood spilled out as he groaned in agony.

"Tell. Me. Where. She. Is." Cian punctuated each word with a brutal punch. The rage consumed him like an inferno. Hot, fierce, and uncontrollable.

"The last I saw they loaded her into a car with your old man," Danny choked out as he hunched over, blood dripping from his face onto Cian's hardwood floor. "He has her, I don't know where. He's going to use her to control you."

Cian looked at the pathetic sack of shit he'd trusted with everything most important to him in the world...

And brought his fist back one last time.

**

Robbie heard the back door to the kitchen open and smiled to himself. "I expected you nearly an hour ago." He held a glass of whiskey above his head. "You could probably use a drink. Come help yourself."

When there was no response but the sound of

footsteps behind him, Robbie shrugged lightly and took a swig himself. He wasn't necessarily surprised by the cold metal ring of the gun barrel that pressed to the back of his head, but he hadn't been sure it would happen either.

"I'm shaking in my boots." His tone was sarcastic, and he took another swallow of his drink.

"Where is she?" Cian growled.

"Someplace safe." Robbie heard Cian's weight shift behind him and then the click of the safety on the gun releasing. Huh. Maybe the kid had a little more to him than Robbie thought.

"You remember the night you made me kill Uncle Dylan?" Cian asked.

Robbie didn't answer.

"You remember how he told me he forgave me, and to go ahead and listen to my Pop?"

Robbie flexed his fingers on the table, discomfort knotting inside him when he thought of his old friend.

"I only remember a scared little boy who refused to become a man," he snapped at his oldest son.

Cian snorted. "I knew right then and there that Uncle Dylan was ten times the man you'd ever been. He sat in that chair without making a sound and let me kill him. He had the grace to absolve you and me, and go to his maker with a clear conscience."

"His maker," Robbie scoffed. "Him and his goddamn religion. Always judging everyone, begging forgiveness for the things that gave us the power to become who we are today. While he was praying the rosary, I was out getting us territory. While he was in confession, I was in every bar, restaurant, and bodega in this neighborhood making sure they knew who was in charge, taking protection money, building a business that's kept you and your brothers in fancy clothes and fancy cars your whole lives."

The gun pressed harder into Robbie's scalp, and he stiffened just a touch, wondering how close Cian really was to pulling the trigger.

"I don't give a shit about the money. I'm not sure I ever did. All I've ever wanted was my family. But as much as you talk about family, you have no idea what it really means to have one. You bullied and threatened and beat us to get your way, and I realized that night with Uncle Dylan you never loved us, just like you never loved him. We were all just pawns. I'm not sure what would have happened if you'd had girls instead of us. Maybe you'd have left them alone…or maybe you'd have whored them out to get yourself more power. Regardless, for you, family's just another word for weapons, and I've been the most important one in your arsenal."

Robbie's heart beat a bit faster as he felt the tension crawling from Cian's hand down his neck and then his back. For over half a century, Robbie MacFarlane had honed his instincts, and at that moment, they told him that he might have finally pushed Cian too far.

"You'll never find her without me," he warned.

"Don't bet on it."

"Your mother—"

"Will never know I was here," Cian answered.

Robbie's heart gave a lurch then, and he moved to stand from the chair, tried to face his oldest son before it was too late, but there was a whispered curse in the darkened room, and then a strange crunch as pain rocketed through Robbie's skull right before everything in his world went completely black.

**

Cian walked briskly through the early morning chill to the nondescript sedan. He checked the surrounding parking lot before sliding into the seat on the passenger side.

"Things didn't quite go down as promised last night," Don said, one eyebrow raised.

"But you got the body and the USB drive, so you can go after the Russians," Cian answered.

Don adjusted the rearview mirror, doing some sort of silent communication with Bruce, who sat in the backseat thumbing through his phone in feigned boredom. "We did, and we will. But I imagine you're more concerned about what the CPD nabbed—he's about six feet tall, green eyes, Irish surname."

Cian gritted his teeth at the smirk on the man's face. "You know I have everything you want to shut down the Dublin Devils, and that I'll only give it to you if Finn walks."

Don's gaze narrowed. "And are we really supposed to believe Liam's lying at the bottom of Lake Michigan even though we found Sergei and his men slaughtered at the whorehouse?"

"You can believe whatever you'd like, but my brother is gone, and you'll never see or hear from him again."

Bruce leaned forward next to Cian's ear, suddenly anything but bored. "A private jet took off from a private airstrip last night. It had filed flight plans for Florida but never showed up and hasn't been heard from since."

Cian let his eyes shut briefly. He could hide the smile that wanted to spread across his face, but he couldn't do it and maintain his stoicism. He was just too damn tired.

"I don't know anything about a private jet. All I know is my brother is gone, and if you want me and the MacFarlane organization, you'd better get Finn out of jail quickly." He turned and looked Don in the eyes first, then Bruce. "You can have me, and I'll serve up myself up on a platter along with a list of evidence so large you'll spend the next decade doing nothing but listing the charges against me. But I need two last things—immunity for Finn, and seventy-two hours to clean up some personal business."

His head throbbed as he thought about where Lila might be and what his father's men might be doing to her. But he swallowed it down and breathed deeply, exhaling slowly as he waited to hear a response.

"You can have your seventy-two hours," Don answered curtly. "But we hold on to Finn until then."

"He has a bond hearing this morning—" Cian began.

"He'll be ordered held without bond," Don interrupted. "He's a flight risk."

Cian nodded. It was to be expected. No judge was going to grant Finn release with the FBI recommending against it. "All right, then, you have Finn as collateral, and I'll be in touch within seventy-two hours."

"What about the old man?" Bruce asked.

Cian's jaw locked like iron. "He won't be

giving you any trouble. Do we have a deal?"

Don glanced at Bruce in the rearview again, and they seemed to come to a conclusion. "It's a deal."

Cian reached for the door handle immediately, desperate to get out of the car and start the search for Lila.

"MacFarlane?" Don asked as the door swung open.

Cian turned and looked at him.

"You're not going to off yourself or something to avoid going to prison, are you?"

Cian snorted in derision. He looked out the window for a moment, then climbed out of the car, leaning down to look at the two federal agents. "Not a chance." *I have far too many scores to settle to leave this earth yet*, he thought.

He slammed the door, and walked away. Cian MacFarlane wasn't done, and he never would be as long as the woman he loved was out there. He'd find her, he'd protect her, and then he'd make sure anyone who'd touched her paid…permanently.

THE END

About the Author

Selena is an award-winning, USA TODAY bestselling author of Thrillingly Ever Afters and a teacher of English as a second language to students around the world. She's a coffee lover, community builder, and world changer who lives in the mountains of Colorado with her family and her goldendoodle. Her favorite city is Edinburgh, her favorite color is purple, and her favorite shoes are Converse.

Selena's books have won the national Reader's Crown award and the Bookseller's Best award, and finaled in the Award of Excellence, the Holt Medallion award, the I Heart Indie award, the Kindle Book Review award, and the InD'tale awards.

When not writing or teaching, Selena volunteers with preschool children at her local refugee assistance center, and dreams of new ways to change the world one word at a time.

6819

CPSIA information can be obtained
at www.ICGtesting.com
Printed in the USA
BVHW08s1429190918
527933BV00031B/1789/P

9 781635 764796